The Faery Sickness

By JennaKay Francis

Writers Exchange E-Publishing
http://www.writers-exchange.com

Dedicated to my father and his "riot of color".
I love you, Dad.

Chapter One

ala Kalei clutched at the medallion about her neck, her eyes closed as if that could block out the sounds coming from the building next door. Soft voices, both commanding and encouraging, grunts of pain, gasps of breath. She shuddered as a sudden scream tore through the air. Then silence. Dreadful silence. Vala opened her eyes, her breath caught in a throat gone dry. Where was the squall of a newborn? The exclamations of joy? She waited for long moment, then sagged at the sound of weeping. The baby had died.

Vala's breath escaped her in a sob, and she threw herself atop the straw mattress in the corner of the shed. Her tears wet the tattered blanket and she hugged close the thin shawl, burying face and heart in the memories it held. It had belonged to her mother, the last woman of this high mountain village to bear a child who had lived.

Vala rolled onto her side, her sobs wracking a body too thin, and too small. All of her prayers had gone unheeded. The sacrifices she had made in the quiet solitude of the woods had gone unanswered. It wasn't fair! But then, the Gods rarely listened to her. If they had, her life would not be so dismal.

Her gaze shifted over the small room's contents, barely visible in the light of a single candle burned too far down. There wasn't much--the mattress, a small table and the trunk taken from her parents' house. Yet, she supposed she was grateful for even the humble room, for it afforded her tenfold more protection than living alone. She shuddered and curled up tighter. Her life had been one dark event after another following the death of her parents.

She had been ten years old when the plague had swept through the village and claimed many lives. She was not the only child orphaned, but she was the most well known. No one had wanted her. Not even her own uncle. He had taken her in only because the church had pressed him to do so, and only until she could find other arrangements. But he had never considered her a human, had always referred to her as fae-spawn, something that had continually mystified her. Her mother and father had been born and raised in this village, had courted here, married here, had started their family here. Had died here.

Yet he had never lost an opportunity to take out his frustrations and anger on her--she had often borne welts inflicted by his walking cane. And he had never lost an opportunity to remind her that she shouldn't have lived, that she didn't belong, that she didn't look like the other villagers.

I do have different color hair and eyes than the other villagers, Vala thought, sitting up. *But how did having blue eyes and blonde hair make her less human?* She leaned against the wooden wall, pulling her mother's shawl tighter around her bony shoulders. The medallion pressed into her bosom, and she pulled the amulet out to look at it. Even in the absence of direct light, the red stone embedded in the silver glistened. The silver chain showed no links, no beginning, no end, yet it moved like liquid against her skin. She stroked it now, taking comfort in the familiar feel. She couldn't even remember when she had first become truly aware of it. It seemed she had always had it, from her earliest memories. The medallion had been a gift from the Outsider, the man who had saved Vala from the faeries.

She leaned her head against the wall and closed her eyes. Her mother had told her to keep the medallion with her always, though hidden. And she had done so, most of the time. Except for that one time when she had placed it in her trunk for safekeeping. That one time. She shuddered, forcing the thoughts aside, and concentrated on the medallion. She turned it over now and silently read the four words inscribed on the back. *Elthea Gannabribriel, Ithys Kjvali.* She had no idea what language they were in, or what they meant, only that she had been forbidden to speak them aloud. Yet, just thinking them, mouthing them, brought her a sense of place, of belonging

Voices brought her alert. Voices she recognized. She turned her head and pressed her ear against the wall separating her room from the others of the house.

"Why, Revered?" Tyrs, the father of the child, spoke. "Lawanda is healthy, strong. Why did our child die?"

A woman, most likely one of the elderly birth attendants said, "The faery sickness is--"

"There is no such thing as a faery!" The voice of the Honorable Revered interrupted. His voice was strong, authoritative, and firm. It broached no argument. "There are only demons. And they are at work here to be sure. They have been at work in this village for nineteen years."

There was a long silence, in which Vala's grip tightened on the medallion. She had heard of the Revered's sermons, even though she had not been there. He had denounced the existence of faeries, telling all that fae was yet another word for demons, minions of the devil, antithesis to the one and only God. Yet, for all of his pronouncements, all of his assurances, Vala did not believe his words. There were faeries! She was sure of it! The fae were no more demons than...than she was. Still, she could not explain all of the deaths. She knew only that for centuries the citizens of the high mountains villages had believed in the Faery Sickness, and that the fae had often taken children. Vala's mother had told her it was an act of kindness, that the fae took only the children who were stillborn, or too ill to survive in the world. But in the past nineteen years all of the babies had died. All except Vala, and that was only because of the actions of the Outsider. She had been born blue, with no life, but the Outsider had only to kiss her small lips and she had been wrenched from the faeries' grasp. Some had claimed he was fae, but now some declared he must have been a demon.

The very thought of a demon saving her life left Vala weak and sickened. She shuddered. All was quiet in the adjoining room and Vala surmised that the elders had either left or moved to another part of the house to talk further. She rose, hid the medallion beneath her blouse, pulled the shawl closer, and slipped from her room into the darkened hallway. "Tyrs?" she called softly. There was no answer, and Vala went into Lawanda's room. A candlelamp burned, sending flickering yellow light dancing on the walls and ceilings. Lawanda turned her head, and began to cry, then beckoned Vala closer.

"Oh, Lawanda," Vala murmured and approached the bed.

Lawanda held the infant, swaddled in a soft woolen blanket. Her voice was barely above a whisper. "Isn't she beautiful? Her skin is the color of milk, her hair like the fire in the sky at sunset. And Vala, her eyes are blue. As blue as yours. I know they are." She paused, looking down at her baby.

Vala studied the infant, grief stalling her speech. The baby didn't look frail at all, but rather robust and healthy. She appeared to be only sleeping, her cheeks still pink and warm.

Lawanda curled a strand of red hair around her finger, then closed her eyes. "I am old, Vala. With each child that dies, I grow older. Soon, I will die...my heart cannot stand it any longer."

Seized by anguish, fighting back tears, Vala whispered, "You will not die, Lawanda. I...I'll find your babies and bring them back to you."

Lawanda's eyes opened. "What?"

Vala frowned, but continued. "Well, if the fae have taken them, they must be somewhere. We have given the fae the mortal body for all of the children. Somewhere the soul and body must be reunited. If I could only find that place, I could bring the children home."

Lawanda stared at her as if she'd gone mad, but before she could respond, Tyrs entered the room, holding a mug of steaming beverage. He stopped in his tracks at the sight of Vala hovering over Lawanda.

"Vala?" he whispered, his face pale. "You shouldn't be here. It's late."

"I'm sorry, Tyrs, but I wanted to see Lawanda. And I wanted to give you both my prayers."

Tyrs flinched at the words. "It's late," he repeated. "Lawanda needs to rest. I've brought her a tonic."

Vala moved aside as he approached the bed. He set the mug on the table and reached out for the baby, but Lawanda pulled the infant aside.

"I want to hold her, Tyrs," she said through fresh tears. "Just for tonight. Please."

Tyrs nodded, pressing his lips together. Vala suddenly felt like an intruder and sidled toward the door. Neither Lawanda nor Tyrs acknowledged her leaving.

She returned to her room, closed the door and sagged onto her bed. Her own words came back to haunt her. Why had she said that? What made her think she could gain access to the Faery Realm? And what if, by some remote chance, the Revered was right? What if demons were taking the children instead of the fae? She shook her head and started to lie back on her bed, but was stopped by a knock on her door. For a moment, she hesitated. Fear plucked at her, and she pushed it aside with difficulty. She was safe here. Tyrs and Lawanda were her friends. They wouldn't let anything happen to her. She rose, crossed the room and opened the door.

Tyrs stood there, his face set with grief and anger. Vala backed away, her heart beginning to pound.

"Wh...what is it?" she managed.

He did not enter the room, but stood silhouetted by the candlelight behind him. It made him look larger than life, more imposing, more frightening. "I want you to leave, Vala," he said, his voice tight and controlled.

Vala gasped. "Why? What did I do?"

His hands rolled into fists at his sides. "Lawanda brought you into this house to protect you. We trusted you. But you have belied that trust. You must leave."

"I don't understand," Vala cried. "How have I belied your trust? What have I done?"

Tyrs grew rigid. His voice cracked when he spoke. "I must relinquish yet another child to the faeries, Vala. I thought...I thought pleasing you would make things different for us. I thought perhaps you would show gratitude. You have not. You must be gone by morning. Take what you will from the larder, but leave." He turned and strode away. A moment later, the lights from the hallway were extinguished.

Vala stood gaping at the open doorway. No gratitude? How could he say that? She had taken the position as servant to Tyrs and Lawanda. She had done everything in her power to show them how much she appreciated what they were doing for her. She had asked for little more than what was needed to survive and sometimes not even that.

She turned his words over in her mind. What had he meant by wanting to please her? That pleasing her would make things different for them? A knot began to form in her stomach. She started as the candle suddenly sputtered, then went out, plunging her into darkness. She had no more wax, and judging from what Tyrs had said, she wouldn't be needing any. Darkness surrounded her, pressing cold fingers against her skin. Fear crept in, and she fought it aside.

She sank onto the floor near her trunk, one hand resting upon it. Leave? Where would she go? She had no money, no relatives. How would she survive? How would she protect herself?

Her thoughts spun to what had happened in the woods with several of the village boys. The night she had forgotten her mother's warnings, the night she had left the medallion at home. She tried to think of something else, but the harder she tried, the easier she failed. Sitting in the darkness made it too real, and terror washed over her--terror as fresh and raw as it had been on that fateful eve.

Tears broke through, and she huddled against the trunk, shaking. She could not get the images from her mind. She saw again the boys' lust-filled eyes, their predatory grins, felt their hands on her, heard their taunts. They were going to have a demon-spawn, see what it was like. It hadn't mattered to them that she was not even a woman yet, that she was a child of just twelve. She hadn't even fought them, too frightened of further retaliation. The physical pain had been excruciating, the emotional pain unbearable.

She shuddered and pulled the medallion from beneath her clothing. She pressed the metal, warm from her skin, close to her cheek. It soothed her, pulled the pain from her, cleared her thoughts. Somehow she knew that not having it that night had cost her dearly. It was a lesson she had learned well from. A lesson she would not forget.

With a heavy sigh, she opened the trunk. There were few things inside, but they were important to her. She moved from memory alone, drawing out her father's clothing and his sheathed dagger. She changed clothes in the dark, replacing skirt and blouse with heavy woolen trousers and shirt.

Suspenders held the pants up, but the legs were far too long. She used the sharp edge of the dagger to remedy that. The cuffs of the shirt she rolled. She had no boots, only the soft leather shoes she wore inside. They would have to do.

Her hair was long, in the fashion of the village women. She gathered it into one hand, then before she could change her mind, she drew the knife through it, severing it just below her shoulders. She stood for a moment, her despair threatening to engulf her, then glanced about the room for someplace to hide the locks. Finally, she gently placed them into the trunk beneath her mother's apron. No one would look there. A snug fitting wool cap went on over her head, her hair tucked up inside, and an old waterskin hung from one shoulder.

Satisfied that she could now possibly look the part of a young boy, she crept from the room and down the hallway. She paused momentarily in the kitchen, wondering if she should take some food as Tyrs had said, then decided against it. The pain of his rejection stung. She would take nothing more from him. She filled the skin with fresh water before opening the back door, and stepping outside.

The door closed behind her, the latch clicking with a strange finality. Darkness pressed against her, and for a moment she froze, fear consuming her. She drew several deep, steadying breaths and stepped away from the house. The moon was full, shedding cold, white light on the lands, and Vala walked quickly, keeping to the darker shadows of the buildings and brush. Most of the villagers were asleep, but she could hear music and laughter coming from the pub. No doubt the village youth were imbibing, oblivious to others' pain and grief. Vala gave the pub a wide berth, wishing she could have found another way out of Strander than past the drinking establishment.

She slipped into the alley behind the building, bent low, slinking beneath the open windows, keeping out of the light spilling to the outside. Just when she thought she'd made it, a figure stepped from the shadows to block her path. She stumbled to a stop, her breath catching in her throat. Her uncle stood before her, eyes narrowed, hand tight about his walking staff. She took a step back, her heart pounding.

"So," Odig snarled, stepping forward. "You're leaving?"

Vala gasped, too terrified to do anything else. How could he have seen through her disguise so easily? And yet, how could he not? She was the only person in Strander with her coloring. Donning a disguise would not mask that. She took another step back, as Odig's gaze flicked over her, seeming to assess every inch of her. It was something she'd endured before, but something she'd never gotten used to. She had learned not to move, not to make any indication that she held anything he might have been searching for, whether it be a bit of stolen bread crust to tamp her incessant hunger, or a chunk of pilfered wax to light the cold darkness of her room. Odig had found them all, and she had been punished severely many times over. Now, she remained as if frozen, her heart pounding, her breath fogging in the cold night air. She was very aware that the only thing she had that might intrigue Odig was the medallion. She had worked hard to keep it from his reach in the few years she had lived at his home. She had kept it hidden behind a loose board in her room, only donning it when she left. Except that one time...she shook the horrible memories aside and watched Odig, her senses on the alert.

It seemed an eternity passed before Odig again spoke, his voice cold and hard. "You do not belong here. Go back to the darkness from which you were spawned."

"I am not a demon," Vala protested weakly. "I am your brother's child."

"You are no relative of mine!" he spat. "Vala died the night she was born. You are a demon housed in her body. You have brought nothing but grief on this village." He thrust his walking stick forward, driving the blunted end into her chest.

Vala staggered backward, momentarily stunned. Then her anger abruptly surged forward. "If I am a true demon, Uncle, then why do I not use my powers on you?"

He started, as if he'd never thought of that. He lifted his cane high. "Be gone, demon of darkness! Be gone!" He brought the cane down toward her head.

Vala gasped, instinctively arching her back, getting her head and face out of range of the heavy stick. It slammed against her shoulder instead. She crumpled from the impact, and he came at her again, bringing the cane down in a fierce blow to her chest. The stick hit the medallion hidden beneath her clothing. Red light shot outward, raced down Odig's walking stick, and engulfed him. He staggered backward, his face ashen, his eyes wide. He staggered, and fell to one knee, then suddenly toppled over in the dirt.

Vala scrambled to her feet, terrified and confused. Too startled to do anything else, she turned and bolted. Past terrors pursued her, down the road, across the meadows and into a thin copse of leafy trees. Still, she did not stop, but raced on, stumbling, falling, picking herself up, and always moving on. The waterskin banged and sloshed against her hip as she ran, leaking cold water down her leg.

At last, exhausted, out of breath, she staggered to a stop, using a birch tree for support. Her chest heaved with exertion, her leg muscles quivered. Confusion numbed her. What had happened? What had caused the red light? Shaking, she pulled the medallion from beneath her shirt and looked at it in the moonlight. The large red stone embedded in the silver sparkled. How could it have done that to Odig? What exactly had it done? So much didn't make sense anymore. Not Tyrs' words, not her uncle's, not the strange occurrence with the medallion. Vala shook her head, and returned the medallion to its hiding place beneath her shirt. When she was rested enough to be aware of her surroundings, she gasped.

She had never seen this part of the meadow before. Two huge boulders stood like sentinels, black against a darker background. Puzzled, she straightened, her leg muscles quivering in protest, and walked toward the rocks. As she passed between them, a tingle shot through her body, much like the ripple of excitement she used to get as a child, playing hide and seek. She paused, one hand on each boulder and leaned forward as a gust of wind swept around her. It brought a strange scent, one she had never smelled before. She took a hesitant step forward, then shrieked as the ground beneath her suddenly gave way.

She slid down a steep embankment, clawing and grabbing at anything she could find to arrest her fall. Sharp grass sliced through her fingers, small shrubs broke free in a cascade of dirt and stone, jagged rock cut into her stomach and arms. And still she fell, until at last, she landed on a small ledge jutting out from the bank. She lay still, stunned, one hand still gripping a piece of plant she had pulled free.

A new sound reached her, pounding and roaring in her ears. She struggled to her knees, her head reeling. She had only a second to take in a vast stretch of water, sparkling in the moonshine, before she toppled, plummeting over the side of the ledge to a pool of water far below.

Chapter Two

Vala regained consciousness slowly. Her cheek was pressed into wet sand, and one hand dangled in frigid water. Her stomach churned, then convulsed, expelling volumes of salty water and sending her body into spasms. When she finally ceased retching, she lay still, gasping, and blinking the stinging water from her eyes. She sat up, confused. She did not know this place. It was night, but her surroundings were lit by a full moon. She looked upward at the rugged cliff towering over her. She remembered falling. She remembered slamming against rock and brush. She remembered falling into water. Her hand drifted to her forehead. She felt no gash but she remembered having received one. She appraised her arms and legs and found no evidence of a fall. Yet, she knew it had happened. So, how then was she sitting here, seemingly uninjured?

She turned her head to stare at the expanse of water she had seen earlier. A quiet shushing noise filled the air, and white foamy water crawled toward her on the grassless ground. She scampered backward in terror until the jagged rock of the cliff pressed into her back. But the water came no closer, in fact receding, only to crawl forward yet again. She watched it warily, then began to inch along the rocks, toward what looked like a larger patch of white ground.

As she rounded a rocky outcropping, the breeze brought a strangely familiar scent with it. Soup. She paused, then squealed as cold water suddenly wrapped about her ankles. It sucked at her feet as it pulled back toward the body of water, and she grabbed at the rocks, then bolted forward. She didn't stop until she again was at the base of the cliff, where she cowered, panting. Still, the water edged closer, hissing as it crossed the ground.

"Stop!" Vala cried, holding her hands before her as a shield.

"Who's there?" a boy's voice called through the night.

Vala froze, her heart pounding. She wasn't sure if she should even answer, but at least it was another person. Perhaps he could keep the water away from her. She waited until the water had again receded, then darted toward the voice, praying she would make it before the water again tried to claim her. She near trampled across a small fire pit before she could stop her terror-filled flight.

The boy tending it looked up, startled, then scrambled out of the way. Vala could see him plainly by the yellow firelight and the silver glow of the full moon. He looked younger than she, though he was a bit taller. Thick, tangled curls of white-gold hung to his shoulders, framing an angular, clean-shaven face. A mid-thigh-length tunic of brown wool covered his lithe frame, though his long, thin legs were bare. He snatched up a pair of breeches from a nearby piece of driftwood and glared at her.

"Who are you? Who were you talking to out there?"

Vala swallowed hard, trying to quiet the pounding of her heart. "N...No one. J...just that water."

He gave her a funny look. "The water? You were talking to the water?"

The way he said made her feel foolish, but it did ease some of her panic. He gave her a cursory glance, then shook out the breeches, turned them over and laid them again on the log, to dry by the heat of the small fire. Vala shivered as a brisk wind caught at her, wrapping about her sodden clothing. She could feel the heat of the small fire and moved a little closer.

"Might I share your fire?" she asked.

He paused, then gestured toward another chunk of driftwood. Vala lowered herself warily to the log, her muscles tense, ready to move at a second's notice. She kept one eye on him, the other on the snarling white foam. For a moment, neither she nor the boy spoke.

"Where did you come from?" the boy finally asked.

"The cliff. I fell." She glanced back over her shoulder at the ghostly white of the cliff wall behind her.

"You fell?" He paused, his gaze darting over her as if assessing her for injuries, then he shrugged and sat down. "If you want to dry your pants, strip them off and lay them next to mine," he said. "Do you have food?"

"No," she replied, not wishing to address the first part of his statement.

He frowned. "Then I suppose you'll be wanting some of mine."

Vala quickly shook her head. "No, the fire is quite enough. Besides, I'm not hungry."

He shrugged and looked at the cliffs behind her. "Where did you come from?" he asked again.

She wondered what more answer he wanted and decided to be cautious. "From atop the cliff. Why?"

He rolled his eyes--large eyes, she decided, like a child's--and huffed out an exasperated breath. "I rather figured that much." He studied her through narrowed eyes, as if seeing her for the first time. "Let me see your ears."

"My ears?"

He got to his feet. "Shades! Must you question everything I say?" He leaned across the fire and grabbed for her hat.

She gasped and came to her feet so abruptly her head caught him underneath the chin, driving his head back. He yelped, stepped backward and tripped over the log he had used as a seat. He sprawled on the rocky beach with another yowl of pain, revealing more of his anatomy than Vala cared to see.

She pulled her hat tight and stumbled backward, very nearly falling over her seat as well. She quickly steadied herself as he came to his feet, his blue eyes narrowed in rage.

"You attacked me!" he bellowed.

"No! I...I..." Vala's fear tangled her tongue.

He dabbed at the blood on his lip. "See here!" he cried in fury. "I'm bleeding! I ought to --"

"Enough!" another voice boomed, and the boy whirled.

"Severrani!" he gasped. "Wh...what are you doing here?"

Vala stood, riveted by terror, her gaze on the man approaching. Tall and lean, he wore the same type of brown tunic and leggings as the boy, though a dark cape whipped out behind him. His hair was also white-gold in color but was bound by a leather tie at his nape. His features so resembled the boy's that Vala thought sure they must be father and son. As he stepped close to the fire, the flames reflected off the polished hilt of a sword fastened at his waist. Vala took an involuntary step backward, keeping the log seat between her and the man. He studied her a moment, his gaze seeming to penetrate clothing and skin, as if he read her innermost thoughts. He addressed the boy, although he did not answer his question.

"Put your pants on," he snapped. "You're in the presence of a lady."

The boy gasped, his gaze flying to Vala, and he snatched up his breeches, then leapt behind the man for privacy. A slight smile caught at the man's mouth, but there was little warmth in it. He fixed his gaze on Vala.

"And you are who?" he asked.

"V--Vala," she mumbled.

"And this is your full name?"

Vala's voice was barely above a whisper. "No, but that is the name my father wished others to know me by." She paused, but his eyes remained fixed on hers and, unwillingly, she continued. "My full name is Vala Kalei."

The man seemed startled, but he quickly recovered and glanced at the boy as he emerged, now fully dressed. "This is Aric, I am Severrani. Sit down."

Vala quickly did as she was told. Severrani sat down on the log opposite her, leaving Aric to find his own seat. The boy glared openly at Vala, obviously still upset at having bared himself in front of her. But his questions were for Severrani.

"What are you doing here? Where did you come from?"

Severrani was quiet for a moment, as if considering whether or not he should answer. He chose not to and once again turned to Vala. "And what are you doing out alone at night?"

Vala didn't want to tell him. In fact, she wanted to do nothing more than run, to get as far away from this stranger as she could. But she felt frozen in place, unable to move, and she heard an answer to his question bubbling upward against her will. To thwart it, she bit her tongue; hard. The pain made her eyes water, but stopped her words in her throat. She forced a calm reply. "I have just started a journey. I am with friends. They are down there." She pointed back the way she'd come.

Aric frowned at her. "You said you were talking to the water."

The man leaned forward. "Perhaps you would like to tell me the truth."

"Th--that was the truth," Vala replied, then gasped as a sudden sting of pain raced through her body. She jumped to her feet, spinning, trying to discover the source of the pain. Finally, her gaze went back to Severrani.

"Yes, that was from me," he said quietly. "Just a small touch of magic."

"Magic?" Vala breathed. She swallowed hard, her gaze again going to Aric. He had brushed his hair back, and Vala now saw that the tips of his white ears were slightly pointed. She swung her gaze back to Severrani, her heart pounding. His hair covered his ears but she was sure they were as unnatural as Aric's were. Pure terror shot through Vala. Demons! She backed away, but was stopped by Severrani's voice.

"Sit." The command was not loud, but not to be ignored.

Vala sagged onto the log seat. "Am...am I dead?" she breathed. A warm flush swept over her and she swayed dizzily.

"Dead?" Severrani repeated, as if amused by the question. "Not that I am aware of."

"But...you? Aren't you a...demon?" Vala could scarcely get the words out.

There was a moment of silence, then Aric burst into laughter. "A demon? Are you stupid or something? We're fae!"

Vala stared at him in shock. Fae? The Faery? "But...but you're so big!" She could not stop her words.

Aric started to retort, but Severrani quieted him with a grip to the boy's arm. He regarded Vala thoughtfully. "And what do you know of the fae?"

"Not much apparently," Aric mumbled, then winced when Severrani shot him sharp glance.

Severrani looked back at Vala. "Tell me, what do you know of the fae?"

"Nothing really," Vala whispered, watching the way the moonlight played through his white hair. "Only what my mother told me."

"Speak it."

"She...she said the fae were gentle, kind, that they helped us. But..." Vala drew a deep breath, and plunged on. "But they take the children, too. They're supposed to only take those who will die, but now they take all of them. Why?"

Severrani ignored her question but Aric had one of his own.

"Why are you dressed like a boy?" he demanded.

Before she could answer, Severrani addressed Aric with barely controlled agitation. "You would do well to keep your manners, Aric. You are already in enough trouble as it is. You have failed in your mission. You went there far too early. Not only that, but you left the Gates open and unattended. You allowed this human to come across the threshold. Think how this will set with your father."

The boy paled but stabbed a finger at Vala. "It's her fault! Normal humans aren't in the meadow in the dead of night. And they don't talk to the water!"

Severrani raised one hand, silencing him. His gaze again slid to Vala. "Why were you in the meadow?"

"B...because," Vala stammered. She didn't want to tell him how she'd run, how she'd been banished from her own home, how blind panic had guided her. Then she remembered her promise to Lawanda. "I wanted to go to the faery realm."

Severrani appeared taken aback. "Why?"

"The faeries have taken three children from my friend. I have come to get them back."

"Get them back?" Severrani repeated, sarcasm dripping from each word. "You truly expect to come here, and take back the children?"

Sudden anger and humiliation brought Vala to her feet. "Yes! You've no right to them. They're not yours!"

Anger darkened the fae's face. "No right? We have every right to them. Your people had their chance. We offered them our knowledge and our friendship. Instead we were greeted with hatred, suspicion and death. Do not speak to me about rights, human!" He suddenly stood, towering over her.

Vala stumbled backward, while Aric moved aside, as if he thought Severrani would take out his anger on him. Instead, Severrani abruptly calmed, re-seated himself and skewered Vala with his cold gaze. "The children belong to us now. As do you. Or to be more precise, you belong to Reth Etharid."

Aric gasped, his gaze flying to Severrani, but before he could say anything, the elder fae held up one hand. "It is late, and time for sleep. Aric, bed down." He looked at Vala. "You as well. In the morning, we will go to Kjvali."

Vala sucked in her breath. "Kjvali?"

"What do you know of Kjvali?" Severrani asked her, his eyes narrowing with suspicion.

"N--nothing," she replied. "I have only heard the name."

"From?"

Vala paused, suddenly very aware of the medallion that rested beneath her shirt. It felt hot against her skin, as if begging that she bring it out, show it to the fae. Yet, she didn't want to tell him about it, about the words written on the back. Again she felt an uncontrollable urge to speak, and she realized with a start that Severrani was using magic on her. She clenched her hands, digging her fingernails into the palms.

"I read it somewhere," she said. "But it means nothing to me. It's just a word."

"Just a word," Severrani repeated, his voice flat and empty. He turned away, pulling his cloak tight. "Sleep."

Vala felt the word like a whip, and she quickly obeyed.

She woke, stiff, sore and foggy-headed, wondering if everything had been a bad dream. It took only one look to convince her it hadn't. Aric lay curled on the ground, sound asleep. She was amazed that he could look so comfortable on a ground as hard as rock itself. She reached out and touched the strange dirt. It was coarse, yet silky, slipping between her fingers as if it, too, was made of water. She shuddered, and looked toward the water, relieved to see it was nowhere close to her or the small camp. Severrani stood near the water's edge, his back to her, his cape fluttering out behind him. The water caressed his boots almost lovingly; swirling about them with a gentleness Vala had not experienced herself. Perhaps then, this great expanse of water cared only for the fae. Perhaps she was safer in their company than not.

Vala studied Severrani for a long moment, remembering his words of the night before. *She belonged to the fae.* How many times had she heard those words? It was bad enough coming from her uncle, but much worse coming from a man of the fae. It brought doubt to her stoic denial. Doubt that ate away at her heart. What if her uncle was right? What if by some horrible stroke of fate, she was indeed fae? Or demon? What if these two men were lying to her? What if they were not faery at all, but rather demons? What would they do with her? To her? The mere thought sent shudders down her spine.

She glanced toward a tumble of boulders well at her back. Perhaps she could reach it, hide there, escape while Severrani's attention seemed to be elsewhere, while Aric yet slept. She quietly rose and backed away, her gaze on the fae. She hadn't taken more than three steps when Severrani's soft, cold voice stopped her. "Going somewhere?"

She stiffened as he turned to face her. She was startled to see that his eyes were blue, as blue as the water he had been looking at. The previous night she had thought them dark, almost black. With an expression of detachment he strode toward her. Instinct made her fall back and bring one arm up in a defensive position. He stopped, regarded her in puzzlement, then nudged Aric with his toe.

The boy grumbled and slapped at Severrani's boot, obviously not yet ready to waken. Severrani nudged him harder, and Aric scrambled to his feet, scowling. "Will you stop that?" he snarled.

Severrani ignored him and reached for his pack. "We shall eat, then walk. Kjvali is a fair distance."

"Walk?" Aric questioned, obviously confused. "Why are we --" He stopped at the look Severrani cast him, although a frown etched across his face.

Vala took a deep breath. "What if I don't want to go with you?"

Severrani's eyebrows rose in surprise. "I don't see that you have a choice, human."

"Why?" Vala cried, "I didn't do anything!"

"You are here," Severrani replied calmly, as if that were answer enough.

"And you butted in where you weren't supposed to!" Aric put in. "I was supposed to take that baby. I would have if you hadn't been in the meadow." He took a step toward her, his face twisted with anger. "Now, because of you, the wolves had the baby instead."

"Aric!" Severrani's tone was harsh, and the boy fell silent.

"Wolves?" Vala's knees grew weak at the horrible thought, and she sank back to her log seat, her stomach tumbling. "Wolves? They took the baby?"

"They did," Severrani said quietly.

Vala stared at him, then sudden, hot tears broke loose. "But...I...it...it wasn't even time for burial! It was night!" She rounded on Aric, desperation driving her to seek someone else to blame. "He said you were there, that you left the Gates open. But it wasn't time yet. There was no burial. So, why were you there?"

Aric paled, his gaze shooting to Severrani, but the elder fae merely regarded him quietly, as if waiting for an answer himself. Aric swallowed hard, his mouth twitching in annoyance.

"I...I just wanted to make sure of my placement for the next day," he finally said, his words slow and measured, as if he hoped Severrani would take that as a valid excuse.

"Day?" Vala cried, hope surging through her. "But it's early yet! Burial may not have happened yet. You still have time. You...you can go there now, get the baby before the wolves do." She rose, heart pounding, and spun toward the cliffs. "I'll go! I'll get the baby!"

"Stay!" Again, Severrani's voice was quiet, yet commanding.

Vala remained still, as tears coursed down her cheeks.

"Four days have already passed in your world," Severrani said.

"Four days?" The words left Vala in a hushed whisper, and she closed her eyes in resignation. There was a heavy silence before she spoke again. "I want to go home," she said, then broke into gasping sobs, and fell to her knees. "No, I...I don't. I want to go away. Far away, where no one knows me, where no one can hurt me. No! I want to die! I want to be with my mother and my father!" She surged to her feet, and spun toward the water. "What is that?" she cried, pointing.

Aric frowned, staring at her as if she were mad. "It's the ocean. What did you think it was?"

"And will it take me away with it?" Vala demanded, then, not waiting for an answer, she stumbled toward the foamy water. She remembered how it had pulled at her feet, as if trying to pull her towards it. Now, she wanted it to do so, to take her to its vastness, to take her away from Strander, her Uncle, Tyrs, her guilt.

Severrani's hand on her arm stopped her at the water's edge.

"Let go!" she screamed, and clawed at him. "Let me go! I only wanted to help her! I wanted to come and get her babies back. Then they would leave me alone! They wouldn't blame everything on me! I could show them I'm not a demon! I'm not fae-spawn!" She realized her gasping words would make no sense to them, but she didn't care. She only wanted to be free of her past, of everything that was Vala Kalei.

But Severrani's grip was too strong, too insistent, and he pulled her away from the water and back toward the fire.

"You can't do that," Aric said, his own voice near panic. "I need you! I need you to tell my father the truth, that you were there."

"But I wasn't there!" Vala cried.

"You were! Yes, I went early. Yes, I left the Gates open. That was an accident. But then you came, and I got scared, and I came back. I didn't take the baby. The wolves did." He sounded as upset as she was, his eyes wide with despair. He clutched at Severrani's arm. "Don't let her go back, Severrani. Please. I need her to tell my father the truth! Please!"

Vala saw true terror in his eyes, and she wondered what punishment awaited him. Not that it mattered. He deserved it. Yet...she could empathize with him. She knew what it was like to be condemned by someone who was family. In that moment, her heart went out to the boy, and she turned to Severrani.

"It's my fault," she murmured. "I shouldn't have been there. It's all my fault. I'll take the blame, all of it."

Severrani seemed stunned by her words. His gaze shifted from her to Aric, and back. Finally, he released his hold on her arm, and peeled Aric's fingers from his wrist. "It is no one person's fault," he said firmly. "We will go to Kjvali. All of us. Aric, try to find something for breakfast."

Aric swallowed hard, and turned away, his face pale, his chest heaving with each breath. Vala frowned, not sure how she should feel anymore. She wanted to be angry at Aric, at Severrani, at everything they had done. But she had felt Aric's terror with every fiber of her being. What harm would it do to tell his father it was her fault? It would keep him from getting into trouble. And she could always plead innocence for her part as well, since she had no idea what she had done. After all, it wasn't as if she crossed the threshold on purpose, despite what her intentions had been. She sighed, and turned back to face the water. There was such power here, such life, and she hadn't even known what it was. She felt like a child just discovering her world. She looked at the strange ground beneath her feet, then hunkered down and ran her fingers through the silkiness.

"What is this called?" she asked.

"Sand," Aric said. "Shades! Don't you know anything?"

Vala felt her cheeks redden. "I've never seen this before. I've lived in the mountains all of my life." She straightened and gestured at the ocean. "Does it go on forever?"

Aric snorted, but before he could give her another sarcastic answer, Severrani stepped in.

"No, it does not. It goes to another land."

"How do you get there?"

"We use boats, made of the finest wood, gifted to us by the forests themselves," he said.

She cast him a sidelong glance. "Boats?"

"A vessel that floats on water."

Vala looked up at him surprised. "Have you ever been on a boat?"

"Yes, many times."

"And it can float with a person on it?" She shook her head. Many times she had floated a leaf or a stick in a mud puddle or in an eddy of the river, but she had never been able to make it actually hold anything of weight.

"Yes." His voice was strangely soft.

"Then what's across there? On the other side of the water?"

He stiffened suddenly as he turned away from her. "Nothing. There is nothing there." He strode back to the fire, snatched up the pack and flicked his wrist at the flames. They died instantly, and he turned toward the white cliffs. "Aric!"

The boy leapt to his feet, glowering at Vala. "What about breakfast?"

"We will eat later. Pack up and move. We have wasted enough time."

Aric uttered an epithet, quickly gathered up his things and stomped after Severrani. Confused by Severrani's actions and Aric's reaction, Vala watched them go. She wondered if the fae would forget about her, if she should remain where she was. Still, she had promised Aric. With a grimace of resignation, she followed them. Besides, she didn't know where else she would go.

They walked along the sand for more than an hour, skirting boulders and driftwood. Though she was young and strong, Vala was not used to this type of exercise. Each step through the silky sand seemed to take twice the effort of walking on dirt and grass. Her muscles quivered with fatigue, and when Severrani abruptly turned toward a large rock tumble and began to climb, Vala stopped, staring upward in dismay.

Aric stopped as well and looked back at her. "What's wrong?"

"I'm tired," she answered, sagging onto a boulder. "I need to rest. And my shoes, they're full of this strange dirt. It hurts." She unfastened one of the shoes, and tipped it, watching the sand fall. It glittered in the sunshine, as if she were pouring bits of gold, and she watched, mesmerized.

"Hurry up!" Aric snapped, startling her.

"You go on. I'll catch up," Vala returned softly.

Aric glanced ahead at Severrani, who was climbing steadily, seemingly heedless of their actions, then shook his head. "I can't. I'm not leaving you here." He reached toward her.

Vala let out a squeak of alarm and stumbled away from him, holding her shoe before her like a weapon.

Aric eyed her in puzzlement, then stomped his foot at her. A lopsided grin appeared on his face when she again leapt backward. "What's the matter with you? Are you that scared of the fae?"

"N...no...I..." Vala drew a deep, shaky breath. What good would it do to explain to him? She slipped her shoes back on, and looked up at Severrani, who had stopped to wait. He was appraising her with eyes as gray as the stone around him. She swallowed hard. "I don't want to."

"Don't want to what?" Aric snapped.

"Go with you," Vala replied quietly, her heart pounding. She had never defied a man before, never stood her ground. It left her feeling weak, overwhelmed, unsure.

Aric advanced on her so quickly she had no time to move, and she squealed in terror when he grabbed her by both arms.

"Aric!" The word snapped out.

Aric winced, and shot a quick look up at Severrani. "Coming!" he called, and shoved Vala toward the rocks. "You don't have a choice. Severrani said so. You're our prisoner. Now, climb, and you'd best be fast. Severrani doesn't like humans, especially humans who talk back. Actually I can't imagine why he didn't just turn you into a puddle of ooze the moment he saw you."

Vala swallowed hard. "He could do that?" she whispered, true terror coursing through her.

"He certainly could. He has loads of magic. Powerful magic. You'd best just do as he says--that is, if you want to live. Now, climb."

Vala drew a deep, resigned breath and made her way up the rock tumble, Aric at her heels. It took nearly an hour to reach the top. Once there, Vala collapsed, trembling.

Severrani turned to her. "I suppose you need to rest," he said.

Vala wasn't quite sure what she heard in his voice, but she struggled to her feet mindful of Aric's earlier words. "No," she said quickly. "I can go on."

Without a word, Severrani turned and strode away, his cape flying out behind him.

"Oh, perfect!" Aric growled. "You and your big mouth! Maybe I wanted to rest, did you ever think of that?" In obvious frustration and fatigue, he struck out at her, punching her soundly on the upper arm, much the way a child would.

Still, she stumbled away from him, fear her first response. But when he made to grab her by the arm, all reason left her. She shrieked and swung out in an attempt to keep him away. Her fist met the side of his face in a resounding blow.

He staggered backward and stared at her in astonishment. "How dare you!" he cried. "Do you know who I am?"

Vala had no chance to retort as white-hot pain coursed through her body from head to foot. Stunned, she collapsed. The pain disappeared as suddenly as it had come.

"Enough, Aric," Severrani commanded.

His face red with anger, Aric whirled toward Severrani. "She hit me!" he cried.

"Perhaps she had cause," Severrani countered.

"Cause? She's nothing but a human! You said that all humans were unworthy of--" He broke off with a yelp of pain.

Severrani's face was tight with his own anger as he regarded the boy. "I said, enough!"

Aric clenched his jaw but backed off. Severrani extended his hand to Vala. Terror stricken, she twisted away, tears already blurring her vision. She blindly scampered away, and ran straight into the trunk of a tree. Instinct driving her, she curled up and pressed against the rough bark, tucking her head, keeping her face out of striking range. For a long moment there was only silence. Then Severrani spoke, his voice confused and soft.

"Why do you cower so?"

Vala drew a quick breath, daring a glance up at him. He was regarding her in outright bewilderment. Aric stood beside him, eyes smoldering with anger. It was enough to make Vala avert her gaze once again. Her tears rolled unchecked down her cheeks to drip from her chin. She started violently when Severrani suddenly hunkered down beside her.

"Don't hurt me," she whimpered. "Please."

He regarded her for a moment. "I will not. Nor will Aric." He once more extended his hand toward her.

Emotionally exhausted, Vala fainted.

She woke to a cool breeze that whispered in the branches of the evergreens high over her head. Her body still trembled, was still damp from the sweat her faint had caused, and her stomach was in turmoil. She was afraid to move, afraid to look at Severrani, wherever he might be.

"She's awake," Aric announced, and leaned over to peer down at her.

Vala jerked back from him, and smacked her head soundly on the tree beside her. Aric drew back, and Vala slowly sat up, clutching her head. After a moment the spinning ceased and she dared a glance at Severrani. He sat on the forest floor, his back resting against a tree with a trunk so large it could well have served as a house had it been hollow. When he looked at her, she gasped. His eyes were bright green, as bright as the new leaves on the bushes surrounding him. He got to his feet, brushing debris from his clothes.

"Aric, give her a drink of water and some bread," he said. He glanced at the sky, then back at her. "We have lost much time because of you, human."

For some reason, the last word stung. "Please stop calling me 'human'," she said quietly. "I have a name."

Severrani looked down at her, as if surprised she had dared to speak back to him. Still, he nodded. "Very well. I shall endeavor to call you by your given name."

Obviously still angry, Aric grunted and tossed the waterskin at her. Vala caught it, opened the cork, and took a long drink. It had a strange flavor, unlike any water she had ever tasted. It wasn't sweet, nor was it bitter. It was distinctive, though she couldn't quite describe it. She started as Aric jerked the waterskin from her hands, then held out a thick chunk of dark bread.

Vala took the bread and tore off a small bit. It seemed to melt in her mouth, tasting of hot butter, nuts and honey. The taste and texture surprised her. She had expected anything so heavy to be coarse and unappetizing. She glanced toward Aric, then offered a chance for a truce. "This is very good. What kind of bread is it?"

Aric shrugged. "Brown bread," he muttered and walked away.

Vala hurriedly downed the last bite and got to her feet. Severrani eyed her a moment, then strode ahead to walk beside Aric. Vala followed, eyes downcast. Her head throbbed, and she stumbled more than once. But her thoughts could not be dislodged from her memories of the fae. Her mother had had the strange habit of putting out food and milk for the faeries, of placing small, shiny trinkets aside for their pleasure. Vala remembered on more than occasion helping her mother make a special gift for the faeries, of staying up 'til the wee hours of the night watching and waiting for the fae to arrive. She never managed to stay awake long enough to actually see them, but in the morning the treasure was always gone. And the reward? Her mother's crops grew better than any of the others in the village. Her father's newborn lambs were heartier, healthier than any other herdsman's. And Vala had lived. She had always believed the fae held magic, but she had never dreamed they would use it cruelly. Still, there was nothing but evil in the magic Aric had used on her.

She sighed and looked ahead at Severrani's back, at the long, white hair, the regal posture. He moved with a grace she had never seen before, not even duplicated in Aric, who made frequent side trips into the woods to gather this or to investigate that. She wondered how old Aric was. At times he acted like a child, at others a man of status, commanding respect. At first she had thought he was Severrani's servant but Aric was too sure of himself, too confident to be indentured to anyone.

And what of Severrani? How old was he? His hair was white, but not the white of old age. It held a glow, like that of a full moon. His thin eyebrows were the same color, though no beard stubbled his sharp chin, no wrinkles marred his perfect skin. And what of his eyes? How could she have been so wrong about their color? Yet, she had been sure only that morning they were clear blue. Not that it mattered. It seemed whatever color they were they drew her, commanded her attention, sent butterflies to her stomach. She shook her head, chastising herself for such treacherous thoughts. She should loathe the fae, not be enamored by them. But she couldn't hate the fae, not even him. No matter the hard looks he gave her, the biting tone of his words. She didn't hate him. And she didn't hate Aric. She felt sorry for them both, though for very different reasons. She knew about Aric's pain, about the fear of displeasing those who cared for him. His terror of his father was clearly evident. That sort of pain she understood. But Severrani? There was so much pain and despair behind the mask of anger he wore. It tore at her. She wanted to know what had caused it, how to make it better. But she supposed there would be no chance for that. She was a captive, nothing more.

She wondered what would happen to her when they got to Kjvali. She wondered who this Reth Etharid was. What penalty would she pay for disrupting the taking of a child to faery realm? It couldn't be any worse than the guilt and horror she felt now. Aric's blunt description of what would happen to the tiny body had only made matters worse. Just the memory brought fresh tears to her eyes, momentarily blurring her vision. She stumbled over a rock jutting from the ground, and fell, landing hands and knees in a tangle of nettleweed that bordered the path. With a soft curse, she quickly regained her feet and tried to brush the tiny, stinging thorns from her hands and arms. Aric shook his head in frustration, though Severrani turned, his gaze questioning.

"I'm all right," Vala said quickly, wiping her hands on her pant legs. "I just tripped."

Without a word, Severrani bent and pulled several fronds from a nearby fern. He crushed them in his hands, then reached for her. Vala drew back, momentarily startled. With a scowl, Severrani tossed the rolled fern to the ground and stalked away. Aric grimaced and retrieved the fronds.

"Rub them on the nettle stings," he told her. "They'll take away the burn."

"I know," Vala mumbled. "I...I just didn't expect him to do it for me. He startled me."

Aric huffed out an exasperated breath, shook his head, and followed Severrani. Vala watched them a moment, then rubbed the crushed fern against her still stinging skin. When she looked up, the two fae were almost out of eyesight. Vala chewed on her lip, then spun and walked in the opposite direction. Neither Aric nor Severrani called after her, and she quickened her pace, hoping to be free of them at last. Rounding one of the massive trees, she gasped when she almost collided with Severrani. Shocked, she stumbled backward. Severrani's cold gaze locked onto hers, although he said nothing. Vala whirled and fled.

She ran, skirting brush, trees, rocks and logs, then skittered to a stop with a cry of disbelief. Severrani and Aric stood in the path before her. Again, she turned and bolted. Memories gripped her. The boys in the woods had taunted her so, chased her, let her believe she was to escape, only to block her path time and time again. They had exhausted her, driven her to cold terror, before they had finally caught and raped her. Tears of terror, rage and panic blurred her vision, caused her to stumble and fall more than once, but always she pushed to her feet and ran on. And always, no matter where she turned, there stood Severrani and Aric. Finally, exhausted, sick and spent, she sagged to the ground, sobbing wildly and heaving into the dirt.

"What is wrong with you?" Aric demanded, his voice holding true astonishment.

"It appears," Severrani said quietly, "that we shall camp the night here." He made a move toward her.

Panic seized her and she scuttled backward. "Don't touch me!" she shrieked. "Don't touch me!"

He stopped, clearly puzzled, then nodded, and returned to Aric's side. The boy looked up at Severrani, just as confused.

"What is wrong with her?" he whispered.

Severrani said nothing, but settled down on the ground, his gaze still on Vala. She put more distance between her and the fae, then curled up, watching, always watching, until, at last, exhaustion won out, and she slept.

Her growling stomach stirred her from sleep in the middle of the night. She started, her gaze immediately going to the fae. But they were still where they had settled down, no closer. She curled into a ball, trying to ignore the hunger pains. She had not eaten, they had not wakened her for food or water. Her throat was parched. Her gaze drifted to the waterskin but it was very close to Aric, and she decided against going after it. After all, what did it matter? She was their prisoner. She had thought a great deal on what punishment awaited her at the end of this journey. She would probably be thrown into some black pit or encased in some eternal spell of damnation for her punishment. The mere idea only sent renewed despair through her.

An animal screeched somewhere in the distance, and the wind rustled through the trees. It wasn't a particularly cold wind, but Vala shivered and pushed into a sitting position. Though the moon was near full, the forest canopy kept much of the light from reaching the ground. Her gaze once more traveled over her companions.

Aric lay curled as he had on the beach, almost like a puppy twisted in sleep. Severrani, however, leaned against a tree, wrapped in his cloak, as if always on guard, ready to leap up at the slightest noise. In fact, Vala noticed that one elegant hand rested lightly on the hilt of his sword. He was a handsome man, exquisitely innocent and peaceful at the moment. A thin beam of moonlight cutting through the forest canopy illuminated his white hair, making it glow. His face was smooth, unmarred by emotion. Her stomach did an unexpected tumble, and she winced. How could she be drawn to someone who wasn't even human? Someone who did such atrocious things as condone the stealing of infants' souls? She shivered, pushing her secret desires aside, and studied him more carefully. Who was he? And who was Aric?

Their relationship confused Vala, who had no siblings, no same-age peers. It was an old heartache, one that ate at her heart, brought tears to her eyes. She had nothing, no one. What did it matter that she was a prisoner of the fae, that she faced their punishment? Her only regret was that she would not be able to return Lawanda's children as she had promised.

Cold with more than the night air, Vala lay back down and closed her eyes.

She woke to early morning sunshine and ravenous hunger. Severrani stood nearby, while Aric sat chomping noisily on his bit of brown bread. He caught her eye as she sat up.

"It's about time," he grumbled. "It's a wonder anything ever gets done in the human world if everyone sleeps as late as you."

"It's not that late," Vala replied, glancing at the small patch of sky visible through the treetops. "The sun has only been up for a few hours."

She noticed Severrani's expression of surprise, though he said nothing. Instead, he gestured toward the pack. "You may eat."

Vala shook her head. "I don't want anything to eat."

Severrani shrugged but Vala was sure she saw a glint of concern flash through the green eyes. "We will leave the forest today," he said, rising.

"And go where?" Vala asked.

"Across the meadows to the desert."

"The desert?"

"There she goes again, repeating everything we say," Aric muttered, then stuffed the last bit of his bread into his mouth and washed it down with a long drink from the waterskin.

Vala's mouth puckered, and she involuntarily licked her dry lips. Aric caught the gesture and held the skin out. She ignored the offer and waited for Severrani to answer.

"It is a land of beauty," the fae said, his voice lost in memory. "Golden sand that stretches for miles, broken only by the howl of the wind."

"Is it dangerous?"

Severrani looked over at her. "That all depends. If one knows what one is doing, then no, it's not dangerous."

"But it can be," Aric put in. "Have you ever been to the desert?"

Vala shook her head. "I've never even heard of one before."

Aric stared at her in disbelief. "You've never seen the ocean, or sand, or the desert? Where have you been living? In a cave?"

Vala felt the color rush to her cheeks. "I...I've never been outside of Strander," she admitted.

Severrani turned toward her, his face a mixture of curiosity and anger. "Then you were born there?"

"Yes."

"But how can that be?" Aric asked, squinting up at Severrani. "I thought we took all of the --"

"Aric!" Severrani cut him off with a harsh word. "Repack. We're leaving."

Aric grimaced, but did as he was told, shouldering the pack and draping the waterskin about his neck. His face was set into a scowl, as was Severrani's, and Vala wondered what had set them to anger this time. She rose, and with a resigned sigh she followed the two fae.

At first the walk was pleasant, but when they entered the meadow, with no shelter from the sun, the heat began to wear on Vala. She stopped more than once to wipe her brow, pushing her hair aside and fanning her face with her stocking hat. Her head spun, and her stomach continually reminded her that she had not eaten for many hours. But, what she really wanted was a bath, or at least a place to wash up. Her skin itched with the residue of the salt water, and she was sure her hair was matted and filthy. Still, she could not bring herself to beg Severrani to find a river or a stream just for her. She frowned, wondering why Severrani and Aric showed little sign of having camped outside. They were almost as clean as they'd been the day she'd met them. Even their hair shone as if freshly washed. She must look a true beggar to their lordliness.

When Severrani finally stopped, she dropped her pack and sagged to the ground, exhausted. She lay back and closed her eyes, barely aware of the sweet scent of lavender that wafted up around her. A shadow crossed her face.

"You'd better have some water," Aric said quietly.

Vala opened her eyes to squint up at him. "Why? What point is there?"

He seemed confused by her question. "Because you haven't eaten or drank anything since yesterday. You'll fall over in a dead faint."

"So?"

"So," he replied slowly, "I'm not carrying you."

She started in surprise and irritation. "Is that the only reason it bothers you? Because you might have to carry me? I suppose you could always just drag me along behind you. Or better yet, just leave me to die where I fall."

He grimaced. "You're very strange, even for a human." He moved away.

Vala stared up at the blue sky. Yes, she thought, that's what all of the village elders used to say. She was strange, not of this world, not belonging to the human race. She with the blue eyes and blonde hair, when all others were dark. She with the slight build, the small stature, when all others were robust. She had been unalike, set apart from birth. She began to believe that it had been no kind service the Outsider had done when he tore her from the grasp of the faeries.

And if he hadn't? Would she be living here now? Would she know Aric and Severrani as friends, comrades? Would she be the one going to the meadow to claim the human children? The thought sent shivers of disgust through her. No, she would never do that. She would never tear families apart, turn what should be a joyous occasion into one of sorrow.

Another shadow moved briefly across her vision and she turned her gaze on Severrani. He stood over her, though she could not clearly see his expression with the sun behind him.

"Why are you not eating or drinking?" he asked.

"What reason is there to do so? Perhaps I shall die and save you the work of taking me to my punishment."

"Punishment? Have I said anything of a punishment?"

Vala paused. "Well, no, not exactly."

"Then why do you believe that you will be punished?"

Vala sighed and sat up, then swayed with dizziness. It took her a few seconds to regain her focus. "Aric said I was a prisoner. I just assumed that meant I would be punished."

"Aric has a fast mouth," Severrani said dryly. "Occasionally his brain does not keep up." He hunkered down in front of her and held out the waterskin. "Drink."

She studied him a moment, wondering what was different about him, but obediently reached for the waterskin. The cold, fresh water slid down her parched throat like a breath of life. She drank and drank, until she thought surely the waterskin must go empty, yet when she lowered it, it still bulged. She frowned and handed the waterskin to Severrani.

He took it, then held out the bread. "Eat," he commanded, and she did.

When she had finished, Severrani rose, replaced the foodstuffs in the pack and called for Aric to rejoin them. Vala got slowly to her feet, realizing he had again used magic on her. In her weakened state she had not been able to withstand it. She was annoyed with herself, yet had to admit that the food and drink had given her renewed energy, and she surveyed her surroundings as if seeing them for the first time.

Broad meadows stretched around her, rolling and cresting and rolling again in waves of green. Pink, blue, yellow, white and purple wildflowers created a dazzling display of color, and abruptly Vala knew what had seemed different about Severrani. His eyes were now amethyst, the color of the wildflowers blooming nearby. She shook her head in bewilderment, wondering what would happen to his eyes once the little group reached the desert.

She didn't have to wait long. Just as the sun was setting in the west, Severrani stopped at the top of a rise. Aric and Vala struggled up the hillside to stand next to him, and Vala gasped in astonishment.

As far as the distant horizon stretched a golden sea. The sunlight cast long shadows over the land, touching at peaks and disappearing into shallow valleys. The wind moved easily here, with nothing to block its path. Sand twisted and twirled in tight columns that danced and skipped over the hilltops, then vanished from sight as if plucked away by the very gods themselves.

Severrani turned away and walked back down the grassy hillside. "We will camp here the night," he told them. "Tomorrow we will begin our journey across the desert."

Aric let out a heavy, resigned sigh and followed the fae, but Vala stood still, mesmerized by the exquisite beauty that lay before her. Even if she were to be thrown into a black pit she would take with her the majestic beauty of this strange land she walked in--the ocean, the trees, the meadows and now the sands. Perhaps her memory of all this grandeur would sustain her through times of travail.

"Are you going to stand there all night?" Aric called.

Vala turned and looked down at him. "I think I'll just stay here awhile," she said. "I want to watch the sun set."

"I suppose you've never seen that before either," he mumbled, and returned his attention to the pack.

Vala sank down, then pulled her mother's shawl from beneath her shirt. It caught on the medallion, and for a moment silver sparkled in the sunlight. Vala hurriedly re-hid the amulet, casting a glance over her shoulder at the fae. But neither seemed to be paying her much attention. With a sigh, she laid her cheek against the shawl. Though it was stiff and coarse from the dunking in the seawater, she didn't care. She could still remember when it was as soft as a kitten's fur, still remember sitting on her mother's lap and being wrapped in her shawl and in her love.

Tears pricked her eyes, but she didn't try to stop them. They flowed over her wind-reddened cheeks, and dripped onto the shawl. She had no family, no home and, now, no future.

They started across the desert the next morning before the sun had fully risen. Aric told her that during the day the sandlands could get quite hot, but at night they were deathly cold. Severrani had spent the previous evening tying long, strong grasses into tight bundles, which Aric now carried strapped to the bottom of the pack. Vala assumed that the bundles would fuel a fire to keep them warm during the nights spent in the desert. She wondered how many nights that would be.

She still could not guess why Severrani was taking her to Kjvali. Since he had claimed she would not be punished, she could think of no reason to go anywhere with him. Still, the destination intrigued her. Kjvali. It was written on the back of the medallion. Now that she knew it to be a township, she wondered what the other three words were. Perhaps people? Or titles? Not that it mattered. She was not planning on making her home in Kjvali if she had the choice. But did she?

She shook the grim thought aside and concentrated on her footing. It was difficult at best. This sand was quite different than the sand at the ocean. That sand had been hard for the most part, but this...this slowed her steps and sucked at her feet, as if trying to pull her under, as if it had a depth to it that could not be matched by hard earth. It shifted and moved and changed, and when she looked back no footprints remained to mark her passage. There would definitely be no retracing her steps. And since Severrani and Aric had all of the food and water, she was dependent on them. She grimaced. Just as she had been dependent on Tyrs and Lawanda. And what had it brought her? Rejection. She wasn't sure she wanted to depend on anyone anymore. And certainly not the fae. However, at the moment, there was no other option. No other choice. She winced. Aric had said she had no choice but to follow Severrani. Apparently he was right. She glanced to her left at the boy.

He seemed to be struggling as well, his face red and sweaty with exertion. He grumbled under his breath about the fact that they were walking, about the searing heat, and about the added weight of his pack. Vala wasn't sure what he meant by that and didn't have the energy to ask.

Severrani alone moved easily, as if unhampered by the deep sands, the weight of his pack or the increasing warmth of the sun as it continued its climb into the brilliant blue sky. Vala hadn't had a chance to look at the fae's eyes yet, but she was so sure they were a golden brown that she was not surprised when he finally did turn to look at her.

"We shall stop to rest," he declared. "It is unwise to walk during the hottest part of the day. Aric, remove the blanket from the pack. Use the two rocks to anchor it against this hill, then support the other ends with the sticks."

Aric nodded, dropped the pack and set to work, still grumbling. Vala guessed that the two heavy stones he removed from the pack were the cause of his earlier complaints. She squinted at him through the glare of the sun.

"I could carry one of those stones," she offered. "It would ease your burden."

He snorted at her. "You're human. You'd most likely collapse within one hour of hauling such a weight."

Vala flushed, averted her gaze and caught Severrani's. His brow was furrowed as if in thought, but he said nothing. In a short time Aric had set up shelter. It blocked out the sun, yet allowed what breeze there was to move through. Vala sat in the shade, thankful for Severrani's ingenuity. Maybe Aric was right, maybe she should be grateful for the fae's knowledge.

Neither Aric nor Severrani seemed in the mood to talk, and after a quick lunch, they both lay back to doze. Vala, however, was unable to rest despite her fatigue. When she was sure both fae were asleep, she crawled from the shelter.

The sun burned hot, searing into her exposed skin and the top of her uncovered head. Still, the ragwool cap she had brought was too hot, and she tossed it back into the shelter next to her shawl. Shielding her eyes against the glare of the sun she looked out over the blazing desert. Something not far away moved in the sand. Curious, Vala started toward it. As she drew closer, she saw that it was a small, furred creature almost the same color as the sand. It peered up at her through beady, black eyes.

Vala smiled and hunkered down before it. "Aren't you a wee, cute thing?" she cooed.

The little animal squinted, then sneezed, and brushed one small paw across its nose. It reminded Vala of a kitten, and she giggled, finding something pleasant for the first time in days. The little creature moved closer to her, its little nose twitching in curiosity. Vala hesitantly held out her hand.

The creature abruptly leapt up and grabbed her finger, sinking teeth and claws into her skin. She gasped in surprise and pain and surged to her feet, shaking her hand, trying to dislodge the animal. It hung on all the tighter, and Vala's gasp turned to a cry of panic and agony.

"Let go!" she screamed. "Let go!" She reached out to push it away, but it used its back, clawed feet to tear into her other hand. Vala withdrew with a small shriek, then started when Severrani suddenly appeared at her side.

He knocked the animal away with one swift, hard blow. It hit the sand, rolled and opened a mouth lined with razor-sharp yellowed teeth. The fae's sword flashed in the sunlight, but Vala grasped his arm.

"No, don't kill it! It's not its fault. I frightened it."

The little creature spun and raced across the sands, quickly disappearing. Severrani looked after it, then turned back to Vala, his expression one of pure surprise. She winced and cradled her bleeding finger.

"Come," he said. "We need to get this cleaned as soon as possible."

He took her by the elbow and guided her back to the shelter. Aric sat up, blinking and squinting.

"What happened?"

"She was bitten by a sandshrew," Severrani replied, reaching for his pack.

"It's not that bad," Vala said, sagging to the sand. "It's just a small bite."

"Small!" Aric cried, looking at the bloodied finger. "It almost took the tip of your finger off."

Vala drew a shaky breath, trying to ignore the pain that swept through her hand and up her arm. Severrani grasped her by the wrist, pinned her arm under his and began to stroke her injured finger with firm downward motions, forcing blood to gush from the wound into the sands.

Vala's breath hissed out in pain, and she tried to pull away. Severrani held tighter.

"Stop it!" she cried. "That hurts!"

"And it will hurt more if I do not remove as much poison as possible," he retorted, continuing his work.

"Poison?" Vala felt faint already. Mention of poison only added to her dizziness.

Aric leaned forward. "You'll most likely lose the finger, maybe the whole hand," he said. "If you don't die first."

"Aric!" Severrani snapped. "That's enough! Instead of frightening her, perhaps you should busy yourself with formulating an explanation for your father on your dismal failure at the meadow."

"That wasn't my fault!" Aric cried. "It was hers!"

Vala swayed, nausea threatening. The heat seemed to have increased tenfold, yet a cold chill swept over her as pain swept up her arm. She lifted a trembling hand to wipe the sweat from her forehead.

"Am I going to die?" she whispered.

Severrani raised one eyebrow as if amused by her question. "No, not if I can help it."

"And if you can't?" she murmured.

"I can," he replied, then removed the bandage, checking to see if the bleeding had stopped. Satisfied, he selected a small tin from his pack, opened it and sprinkled a fine, yellow powder across her open wound.

Fiery pain leapt up her arm, raced through her shoulders and shot to her head. She clenched her teeth to keep from screaming. Aric watched her carefully, as if anticipating she would faint again or shriek in agony. She was determined to do neither under his scrutiny. Apparently her silence surprised him, for she saw the unmistakable look of awe settle in his eyes. It heartened her. For once, she had done something other than incur his sharp tongue.

Severrani drew out some clean bandages and re-wrapped her finger securely, then handed her the waterskin, encouraging her to drink with only a glance. She drank her fill, though her hand trembled. Severrani glanced at the sky before settling back in the sands, now made cool by the shade of the blanket.

"We shall stay here until evening," he said.

"Evening?" Aric cried. "But that means we'll only have a few more hours to walk before it gets too dark too see."

"And are you that anxious to return home, Aric?" Severrani asked, his voice soft and curious.

The boy flushed. "Well, no, not really. But it wasn't my fault. It was hers. And once I show him the cause of my failure, I'm sure he'll understand."

Vala blanched, her gaze darting to Severrani, who addressed Aric thoughtfully.

"Do you think so?" Severrani asked. "And do you also think the Reth will take out his disappointment on Vala?"

She regarded the fae in surprise. That was the first time he had said her name, and she rather liked the way it rolled from his tongue. But she didn't like the question he had posed to Aric and waited for his answer.

The boy studied her, his gaze critical. A frown crossed his face, and he drew his mouth into a tight line. Severrani gave a small, grim smile.

"So," he said quietly, "you only now see the probable outcome of this meeting?"

Aric blanched and surged to his feet. Without a word to either of them he strode from the shelter, his pace fast and furious. Severrani didn't try to stop him, just watched him go, although the depth of sadness in his eyes made Vala wince.

"Why does that upset him?" Vala asked. "My meeting with his father?"

Severrani was quiet for a long moment. "Aric's father will not allow him to use you as an excuse. He will be punished."

Vala swallowed hard. She had seen the fear in Aric's eyes earlier, had seen it every time Severrani had mentioned his father. She looked up at the fae.

"Does his father beat him?" she asked softly.

Severrani started. "No! Of course not!" he said, but there was little conviction behind it. He rose and moved away.

Vala frowned. "What did you mean by 'probable outcome of this meeting'?"

Severrani shrugged. "I would think that's obvious. You will belong to Aric's father."

"What!" Vala cried, her cheeks flaming. "I will belong to no one, certainly no man."

A small smile played across Severrani's lips. "Reth Etharid is not a man," he said softly.

Fear swiftly replaced Vala's embarrassment. "Fae, then!" she cried. "Still, I will not be owned by him or any other! If that's the reason you are taking me to Kjvali, you may as well consider this journey over!" She could not stop the pleading tone in her words, could not stop her trembling at the very thought of another man touching her.

Severrani chuckled softly, his golden eyes flecked with sadness. "You, human, have little say in the matter. The moment you set foot in our world you became his property."

"I don't believe that." Her voice was no more than a husky whisper.

"It doesn't matter what you believe. It matters only what the law states. Here, fae law, not human law, governs you. Here, you belong to the Reth."

"I'll not stay with him," Vala retorted. "I'll leave."

"Then," Severrani said, "you will die."

The night passed excruciatingly slowly for Vala. The trio had continued on for several hours before night robbed them of light. Now, after a torturous rest, in which her hand throbbed with pain, her heart was in turmoil. She didn't want to believe that Severrani was actually going to hand her over to this Reth person. After the way he had rescued her from the sandshrew, the way he had gently treated her wound, the sadness and loss in his eyes...She shook herself. Yes, she was drawn, for some inexplicable reason, to him. But she could not delude herself that he would reciprocate the feelings. Aric had said Severrani disliked humans. There was no reason to believe any differently. Still...he ignited a fire within her at the simplest touch. A fire she had never before known, most likely never would again. She had thought the boys in the woods had killed any emotion inside her. Yet, when Severrani spoke her name, it seemed to take on new meaning, new emotion and depth. It sent butterflies to her stomach. She yearned to hear him speak it again.

She sat up slowly, cradling her injured hand with the other. It hurt. A lot. Her gaze slid to Aric. He had trailed Vala and Severrani the previous night, said nothing to either of them and promptly curled up to sleep once they stopped. He slept still, and once again Vala was captivated by the sweet innocence of a fae's face. There was something at once mystical and enchanting about it. Only when they were awake was she witness to the bitterness that marred the fine features and hardened the thoughtful eyes. Eyes that she could easily sink into, given the chance. She sincerely hoped that Severrani was telling the truth, that Aric's father would not beat him. Vala didn't want the guilt of such a punishment on her heart. With a sigh, she turned away and stood.

"And you are going where?" Severrani's voice came, cool and soft.

Vala's pulse quickened at the sound of his voice, but she avoided looking at the fae as she answered. "I have personal needs to attend to."

"Do so, then," he said, then added, "But please, no more offering of fingertips to sandshrews."

His teasing words did nothing to thwart her sudden arousal. His voice was like silk, draping around her with cold richness. She kept her tone equally cool and detached when she responded. "From what I understand of your great power, healing a sandshrew bite is nothing."

"Oh? And just where did you learn of my 'great power'?"

She finally turned to look at him, surprised to see that his eyes were now a dark blue, the color of the blanket that provided shelter. For a moment, she forgot the question as she stared into their depths. Severrani's small smile jolted her into speech.

"Aric told me. I would think that if you are capable of melting someone into a puddle of ooze, healing my finger would be quite easy."

"A puddle of ooze?" Severrani broke into quiet laughter. "Never have I turned anyone, human or otherwise, into a puddle of ooze. Do humans believe everything they hear?"

Vala felt color warm her cheeks, and she turned away from him, stung. She would not dignify his teasing with a response, not let him see how much it had hurt. She hurried away from the shelter, climbed a rise in the sand and slid down the other side. Seeing no place of privacy in the barren landscape, she quickly relieved herself, knowing neither Severrani nor Aric would intrude.

For a moment she considered walking off in the opposite direction, but abandoned the thought as the early morning sun beat down relentlessly upon her bare head. She reached up and tried to pull her fingers through the tangles in her hair. But it was impossible, and at last, she gave up in frustration.

I shouldn't have cut it off, she thought. *At the least I could have braided it. Now...* She paused, abruptly remembering the old dagger she'd slipped into the pocket of her trousers. She reached for it, wondering that she had not thought of it before, but it was gone, slipped out through a hole the size of her fist. She stood, mouth open in disbelief, then suddenly a giggle welled up inside of her. Try as she might, she could not tamp it down, and she fell to her knees, shaking with laughter, born of despair and resignation.

Independent? Her? How preposterous to even think that? She hadn't even felt the dagger fall free. It was probably lying on the floor of her room back in Strander. And the waterskin she'd taken--that had already leaked almost dry. She had left Strander with no food, no weapon, and no plan. What a fool! How could she ever expect to survive on her own? She was a child who had never learned how to grow up.

So, maybe it was time to try. She sat back on the hot sand, ignoring the sting as it burned her palms. She supposed she could try to slip away. She would never make it on her own in the sandlands, but perhaps when they once more entered a forest or a meadow she could slip away. The problem was, did she really want to? She could not seem to tear her thoughts away from Severrani. Why? What was so special about him? After what had happened with the boys in the village, she had been fearful of all men. Why? Most of them could no more fight than...than cook! Yet, Severrani was fae, he had magic, power, and he looked as if using a weapon came easily. And she was not frightened of him. A sudden thought occurred to her--magic. Was he using his magic on her? Using it to seduce her, bind her to him? She supposed that would be a very effective way to hold a prisoner, by making them want to stay. And how could she fight magic? Her shoulders sagged in defeat. She rose, trudged back up the hillside and returned to the shelter. Aric was awake, glowering as usual as he munched on his breakfast. She wondered what he looked like when he was happy and content.

"What did you do to your hair?" he asked.

"Nothing," she replied. "Why?"

"It's white."

"White?" Vala reached out to pull a tangled strand forward. It didn't look much different to her and she shrugged. "No, it's not. It's blonde, but not white."

Aric shrugged. "Well, on top it is." He chuckled suddenly. "You're starting to look like a fae yourself."

Vala's hand fluttered to the top of her head, her breath caught in a throat gone dry. "No," she whispered. "I'm not." She shot a frantic glance at Severrani, hoping he would negate Aric's words.

But the elder fae said nothing more than, "Are you ready to go?"

"No!" Aric cried at once. He shoved the last bite of brown bread into his mouth and took up the waterskin, drinking from it long and noisily.

Vala paused, then reached for her own waterskin. Under Severrani's curious gaze, she opened it and tipped it slightly. Nothing came out. She tipped it farther, and a last tickle of warm, stale water spilled into her hand. With a grimace, she attempted to clean her face.

"That's disgusting," Aric said, wrinkling his nose.

"You would do well to follow her actions," Severrani told him, pulling the waterskin from his grasp. He took out his kerchief, dampened it and handed it to Vala.

Surprised by his actions, she accepted the damp cloth and wiped her face. The cold water made her skin tingle pleasantly. She dabbed at her neck as well, though what she really wanted was a bath. She looked back at Severrani.

"How is it that your water is always cold and plentiful, while mine is hot and evaporated due to the heat?"

He shrugged, but Aric answered.

"Magic, of course."

"Magic," she echoed, then shot him a quick glance, expecting him to comment again on her tendency to repeat words.

If he had intended to say anything, Severrani's look stopped him. Aric took the waterskin back, poured a bit of water into his hands, then scrubbed at his face, doing little more than smearing the dirt from his hands onto his cheeks. He looked like a child caught playing in the mud. Vala couldn't help smiling.

"What's so funny?" Aric demanded.

"Nothing," Severrani interrupted, rising. "Pack up. We need to move on."

"You know, I'm getting a little tired of being the servant around here," Aric retorted, his gaze on Vala. "Why can't she do something?"

"I offered, remember?" Vala pointed out.

"Well, offer again, then," Aric said, his tone challenging.

Vala stiffened, knowing he was baiting her. "No." Her calm retort surprised even her. She wasn't use to speaking back to anyone, men in particular.

His eyes went wide, and his face reddened with anger. He surged to his feet, but before he could throw either magic or fist her way, Severrani gripped his arm. Although he kept his gaze on Aric, he addressed Vala.

"You will help," he stated. "There is no reason for Aric to do all of the work."

"I don't have a pack," Vala pointed out.

"You will use your shawl. It is quite adequate to carry the grass bundles and the food. Aric will carry the rocks and the blanket. I have the water."

Vala hesitated a moment, then placed her mother's shawl on the ground. With a defiant glare at both of the fae, she picked up one of the rocks, placed it at the center of the shawl, then lay the grass bundles over that. The food rested on top. Once the ends of the shawl were pulled together into a knot, the shawl made a serviceable pack. She slung it over her shoulder and waited.

Aric said nothing. He merely shrugged, packed up the blanket and the remaining rock, and rose. Severrani watched the preparations quietly, holding his own small pack over one shoulder. When the packs were completed he gestured Vala and Aric forward. Vala fell back a step, again examining the ends of her hair. She didn't want Aric to be right, but even she could see that her hair was no longer blonde. It was white. *It's just the sun,* she told herself. *The sun is baking the color out. That's all it is.* But even to her, the words rang hollow.

Chapter Five

They walked until the sun reached its highest point. Vala was exhausted, overly hot, sweaty and in pain. The rock she was carrying was heavier than she'd thought, and her shoulders ached. Plus, her finger continued to throb, sending pulses of agony all the way up her arm. She remembered Aric's words about the sandshrew's bite being poisonous. The idea sent morbid thoughts racing through her mind. She didn't want to die. Not really. And certainly not a slow, prolonged death due to illness. She still wondered if Severrani had the power to heal her finger, if he was withholding it because she was human and not fae. The possibility gnawed at her, fanned the flame of her anger, so that by the time they stopped for rest she was in a foul mood.

She shucked off the shawl-pack, and flung the stone toward Aric, narrowly missing him. He yelped, then moved toward her in anger. Severrani stopped him with a firm grip. Vala glared at them, then stomped away. She hadn't taken but a few steps when she felt Severrani's hand close about her upper arm. She gasped, and immediately tried to pull away, but his grip was firm and unyielding.

"What do you want?" she cried. "Let go." Old fears resurfaced with a sickening rush.

"I need to look at your injury," he replied, his voice soft and soothing. Curiosity narrowed his eyes, but he did not press Vala for answers on her sudden fear.

"Why? What for? You've done everything you can for it."

"I will look at it just the same," he said and led her back to the shelter that Aric had already constructed. "Sit down."

She warily dropped to the ground. Severrani sat down across from her and opened his pack. He took out the waterskin and more of the yellow powder he had applied to the wound earlier. Vala balked, clearly remembering the burning pain it had caused. Already she felt hot and faint.

"I don't need any more of that," she said quickly and got to her feet, though where she expected to go, she didn't know. The sandlands seemed to be blurring and shifting before her eyes. She blinked and raised a shaking hand to her brow.

"Are you scared?" Aric taunted.

"No!" she retorted. "I just don't see the point. What difference could it possibly make?"

"The difference between living or dying," Severrani replied.

The harsh words startled Vala, and she looked at the bandaged finger. "But it was just a bite. Does that little animal really carry a poison?"

"Some call it that," Severrani answered. "Sit down."

Vala's legs buckled, and she sank down onto the sand. Severrani took her hand and gently unwrapped the bandage. Vala winced as it stuck, then sucked in her breath when the fae loosened it with a wash of water. Using another piece of cloth, he dried the skin, then leaned forward to examine it closely.

His head came within inches of her face, and she breathed deeply of his essence. She would have expected him to smell of sweat and dirt. Instead, she caught the scent of spice, or mint, or...she couldn't decide, but it was pleasant. Too pleasant. Almost against her will, her free hand strayed upwards and touched his white locks.

He raised his head to look at her, and she snatched her hand away, embarrassment flaming her cheeks. He said nothing, but his golden eyes glowed with amusement. Vala averted her gaze, then caught Aric's smirk and closed her eyes.

A moment later searing agony brought them open again as Severrani again applied pressure to the wound. Vala struggled against his hold, as blood spurted from the wound to drip into the sand. "What are you doing?" she cried.

"It is infected despite my medicines," Severrani told her. "I must clean out the infected material so that my powder can work more effectively."

"Well, stop it! It hurts!" She pushed against him with her other hand. "Stop it!"

"Aric, hold her, please," Severrani said.

"Don't you touch me!" Vala shrieked. She tried again to pull free of Severrani, her panic and pain increasing by the second. It was too close to her past, too real. The pain, the terror, the inability to move, to escape. Severrani's hold was stronger than even all four of the boys, and as Aric moved toward her to obey Severrani's command, Vala swung out with her fist, determined to keep him away.

He ducked, and Vala's hand hit the side of Severrani's head with a solid thwack. He reeled back, shock evident on his face. As his eyes met hers, Vala froze. Self-recrimination snuffed out her panic, brought reason back with stinging force.

"I--I'm sorry," she stammered. "I didn't mean to hit you. I was trying to hit--" She broke off, realizing how awful the rest of her explanation would sound.

Aric sat back, his gaze moving between Severrani and Vala. Severrani set down the tin of powder with controlled movements, then rose and walked away. Vala stared after him, wondering at the emotions raging through her. She had done it again--hurt him when he was only trying to help. Guilt tore through her, and her tears rolled down cheeks hot and sweaty.

"Let me finish," Aric said, his voice unexpectedly soft.

Though surprised, Vala didn't refuse. She allowed him to sprinkle on the yellow powder, then rewrap the wound, all the while clenching her jaw against the pain, keeping it to herself. When he was finished, he handed her the waterskin.

"You look pretty flushed. You had better drink more water," he said.

"Why does it matter to you? To him?" Vala asked in confusion. "Why do you care what happens to me when I am only considered a prisoner, someone to be turned over to your father?"

Aric paused, darted a sidelong glance in the direction Severrani had gone, then scooted closer to Vala.

"Do you want to go home?" he asked quietly.

She started. "Of course I do! Why?"

Aric hesitated. "I can take you back."

Vala stared at him, confused and wary. "Why? I mean, why would you? I thought I belonged to the fae now."

He shrugged. "Did Severrani tell you about my father? About what he might want with you?"

"No, not really." She hesitated. "Exactly what would your father want with me, anyway?"

Aric almost choked on his disbelieving laughter. "What do you think?"

Vala shook her head. "I don't know."

Aric stared at her in astonishment. "Think about it a minute. I'm sure it'll come to you."

Vala frowned. It seemed she should know the answer, but her thoughts were completely scattered by the throbbing pain in her hand. "I don't know," she finally mumbled.

"Oh, by the gods! Don't you know anything? You'd be his concubine! One of the ladies in his private chambers."

Vala gasped, "No! I...I wouldn't do that!"

"As if you would have a choice," Aric retorted. "Don't you get it? You would be his property. He could do with you as he wished, anytime he wished. You would have no say in the matter."

Vala went cold at the mere thought. She rubbed her forehead, trying to erase her pain and panic. After a moment, her gaze slid again to Aric. "Why?" she asked. "Why would you want me to go home? I thought you needed me to tell your father what happened."

Aric frowned. "It wouldn't matter. He'd still take out his anger on me. At least this way, I win a small victory."

"What do you mean?"

"I deny him you." He looked up as Severrani suddenly appeared on the sandy rise to his left. "I finished treating her wound. Will we eat lunch now?"

Severrani nodded and sat down in the shade. Vala wondered where he had gone, if he had heard anything Aric said. She hadn't had a chance to ask Aric how he planned to get away from Severrani. How did one escape from someone with magic? Or was Severrani's magic limited? He had scoffed at the idea of turning people to ooze, and he hadn't used magic to heal her. So far, all she had noticed were the little pricks and the fact that the water stayed fresh, cold and plentiful. Still, she wondered what he was capable of.

Aric handed her a piece of the brown bread, and she took it, though she scarcely tasted it. She kept her gaze averted, fearing Severrani would be able to read her thoughts. If Aric was successful in returning her home, would

Severrani be able to reclaim her from the land of the humans? Would she be safe there? And what would happen to Aric if he did take her back? Would Severrani punish him? He'd already said his father would, regardless of whether she was there or not. She didn't see the point, then, in continuing on with the two fae. If she couldn't sway Aric's father to forgo any punishment, then why go to Kjvali at all? Thoughts of Aric's father and what he would force her to do made her gag. She turned away, but not before she caught Severrani's look of question. She closed her eyes and willed her stomach to settle.

After the brief meal, Severrani and Aric stretched out to nap until the air cooled, and they could once more begin walking. As before, Vala set out to investigate her surroundings, sleep eluding her. She walked to the top of the first rise and scanned the distant horizon. Sand, shimmering with heat waves, stretched as far north and south as she could see. She turned and looked west. The meadows were no longer visible, nor were the ocean or trees. Undulating hills of golden sand hid them from her view. To the east she could make out the first signs of a break in the desert. Pale green growth hugged the ground, but beyond that the greenery looked more alive and vibrant, almost unnatural in its color.

"That's Larendalath," Aric said, coming up beside her.

Vala started at the sound of his voice, though he spoke quietly. "What's Larendalath?" she asked, looking at him.

"That." He gestured toward the greenery in the distance. "The land of the fae. Home."

"Home? But I thought we were in the land of the fae. Here."

Aric shook his head. "There's a transition zone between your world and mine. Sort of like a barrier to keep people from slipping back and forth too easily. We call it Talede."

She looked at him, puzzled. "Do you mean that humans can accidentally enter the Faery Realm?"

"No, not the realm. Just the transition zone."

"How? I mean, don't they wonder what happened? I knew something had happened straight away."

"Did you? And what were your first waking thoughts on the beach?"

Vala frowned, trying to recall them. Then she regarded Aric with understanding. "I thought I'd had a bad dream."

He nodded. "And usually the human is back in their own world before they ever wake. And they remember crossing to Talede as only a dream, be it pleasant or a nightmare."

"Then why didn't I wake there instead of here?"

Aric shrugged. "That I don't know. Now, do you want me to take you back or not?"

Vala glanced over her shoulder. She could see Severrani stretched out in the shade of the shelter, apparently asleep.

"How? How do we get away from him?"

"That's been taken care of already. We can leave now."

"Taken care of? What do you mean?"

"I do have magic, Vala. Magic I can use. He'll be asleep for hours, maybe even the night."

Vala stared at him in alarm. "But he could get bitten by one of those sand creatures! Or--or something else that lives out here. He can't protect himself."

Aric shrugged. "There's nothing out here, and not many that would be likely to even try to attack him. And even if he did get bitten, he could heal himself. He's got medicine. Besides, my sleep spells don't usually last long. Now, do you want to go or not?"

Still Vala hesitated, her heart pounding. "But what about water? There's only one waterskin. We can't take it from him, and we can't survive without it. And what about the food? And the blankets? How can we survive if we split up?"

Aric frowned. "Perhaps all of your talk about wanting to go home, about not belonging to any man, was just talk, then." He started to turn away. "I'm sure Father will be very pleased with you, as least as long as you live."

The bitter words seared through Vala's mind, brought her up with a little gasp. She grabbed Aric's arm, stopping him.

"I want to go back," she whispered. "I will not be a whore to anyone, be it man or fae. But I don't want Severrani to suffer, either. Are you sure he'll be all right?"

Aric nodded. "I've left him some food, and some water in your waterskin."

"Mine?"

"Well, that only makes sense. There are two of us, one of him. We'll need the magic waterskin. We'll leave him the blanket shelter as well. I've got everything packed already. Let's go."

Vala swallowed hard, then followed him to the shelter. He took up his pack and, without a backward glance, strode away. Vala looked at Severrani, lying so peacefully before her. How would he take her disappearance? Would it matter to him any more than losing a potential slave for the king? It mattered to her, in a way that it shouldn't have. She glanced toward Aric, suddenly just wanting to call the whole thing off. But the younger fae had already disappeared over a rise in the sands. Vala looked again at Severrani, then she bent and shook the grass bundles from her shawl. For a moment, her hand again strayed to his soft, white locks, then with a heavy sigh, she followed Aric.

Aric kept a fast pace, his steps directed south. Vala did her best to keep up, although her legs trembled from the strain of slogging through the thick sand. The sun beat relentlessly on her uncovered head and face. Soon her lips felt dry and cracked. Aric carried the waterskin and she was loath to beg him for water. She still felt guilty about leaving Severrani with her rancid waterbag.

"Why are we going south?" she asked, catching up with Aric.

"We're going to your home."

"But we came from the west," she pointed out.

"I know. I'm not sure why Severrani was taking the long route to get to Larendalath. In fact, I'm not sure why we were walking at all. He could've used magic. We could have been home days ago. At any rate, we'll be back at the meadows by tomorrow night, maybe earlier if we don't stop to rest so often." He cast her a sidelong glance. "You can keep up, can't you?"

"Of course, I can," Vala returned, although she wasn't sure of the truth in that.

"Good." He turned away and quickened his pace, as if he thought Severrani was tight on his trail.

Vala drew a sharp breath and stumbled along after him, his words only just registering. If Severrani had magic to get to Kjvali without walking, then why hadn't he used it? What was he reason for not only walking, but choosing the long route as Aric had pointed out? He had obviously been no less eager than Aric to get home. But why? And, if he had magic, then what was to stop him from using it to find her and Aric? The thought sent strange feelings through her. She both did, and didn't, want him to do so. She shook her head, trying to dislodge thoughts of the fae, and hurried after Aric. He didn't stop until the sun was well down, and only then because it was too difficult to see their footing. Obviously, he was unhappy about having to stop at all, but finally did so with an exasperated sigh.

"We'll rest until it gets light enough again," he stated, dropping the pack.

Vala didn't answer, couldn't answer. She was too exhausted to even think straight, and her whole hand burned with pain. She sank down in the now-cold sands, pulled her shawl tighter, and wrapped her arms about her legs.

"I'm freezing," she managed.

Aric ignored her, and opened the pack. He took out the bread, broke off a small chunk and handed it to her, then took his own.

Vala ate her meal in silence, her thoughts continually straying to Severrani. She wondered if he had awakened yet. And, if he had, what his immediate reaction would be to their disappearance? Would he be angry? Sad? Worried? Or merely dismiss the incident--and her--and return to his home?

She grimaced. She doubted that. Not when he had seemed so adamant about turning her over to Reth Etharid. And she didn't suppose Severrani would simply abandon Aric, either. Somehow, she was sure Severrani would be furious that Aric had used magic on him. Aric must have been just as sure to keep to the pace he'd set. Prior to this he hadn't shown much eagerness to move quickly. Now, he walked as if the twelve demons of the netherworld were on his heels.

Aric finished his bread and washed it down with long swallows of water. He caught her eye and held out the skin. She took it hesitantly, too thirsty to ignore the offer. The water was clean and cold, and again she wondered what sort of magic kept it that way. At the thought, her guilt returned.

"We shouldn't have taken this," she murmured.

"Nonsense," Aric retorted and lay back, although he seemed agitated. He kept swiveling his head, squinting into the darkness around them, as if he expected at any moment that Severrani would appear.

Vala recapped the waterskin and returned it to the pack. "Who is Reth Etharid?" she asked.

"My father," he mumbled.

"I know that much. I mean, who is he? Why would I be his property when I entered this land?"

Aric huffed out an exasperated breath, but answered, his voice low. "Because he's the king, and he owns everything and everyone in Larendalath."

"The king! Then that means you're--" She gasped.

He laughed, though it was without mirth. "Yes, a prince."

For a moment Vala was too stunned to speak.

"Go to sleep," Aric said, lying down. "I'm leaving early morn."

"But if you're a prince," Vala persisted, "then who is Severrani? How can he speak to you like he does? How can he hurt you with magic?"

Aric didn't answer, and Vala lay down as well, though she wanted to shake the information from him. Severrani's words abruptly echoed through her mind: *Do humans believe everything they hear?* She didn't know what to think of Aric's announcement. Perhaps he was only teasing her. She couldn't see how he could be a prince and still answer to Severrani as if he were no more than a servant.

But what if Aric was telling the truth? Then Severrani certainly wouldn't let the young prince simply walk off into the sandlands. He would come after Aric. After her. Wouldn't he? And what mood would he be in when he did find them? The questions still troubled her as she fell asleep.

Aric woke her with the first light of day. The sun had barely crested the horizon; the air was chill. Vala's sleep had been fitful, plagued with cold and bad dreams. In addition, her hand still throbbed, reminding her of the wounded finger. She wondered if Aric had brought the yellow powder and some clean material to bandage the injury. If he had, he made no mention of it. Nor did she, not willing to suffer more pain than she already had.

"Let's eat and be on our way," he said curtly. He regarded the sky, alive with dazzling colors of pink, blue and orange. A slight wind blew across the sands, whistling eerily as it twisted and curled about the golden hills. "I don't like the direction or sound of this wind," he added.

"Why? What does it mean?" She got to her feet, her gaze moving warily over the lands.

"Might mean a sandstorm. I hope not. Anyway, if we're quick we'll make the meadows before it hits."

"A sandstorm? Are they dangerous?"

"Only if you aren't prepared for them." Aric started walking, digging into the pack at the same time. He again produced a chunk of the bread and handed it to her.

"What do you mean 'prepared'?" she asked. "How does one prepare for a sandstorm?"

"Mostly just by being aware of it, knowing that it's coming."

Worry chewed at her. "But Severrani might still be asleep! What will happen to him?"

Aric glared at her. "You certainly seem concerned about him of late. Do you like him or something?"

Vala felt the color rush to cheeks already red with sunburn. "No!" she cried. "I--I just feel guilty about leaving him alone back there."

"Why? He's an adult. An adult with magic. He can take care of himself."

"I know," Vala replied softly, wondering at her own conflicting emotions. "I know." She chewed unhappily on her bread.

Aric cast her another questioning glance, then shook his head, and hurried through his own breakfast. They walked the morning in silence, Vala too winded to even try to make conversation, Aric seemingly not interested anyway. She once more pondered his recent pronouncement of his princely status. Was it true? She studied his back, then shook her head in dismissal.

He was probably nothing more than Severrani's servant, at that. He certainly didn't have the air of royalty. Not that Vala had ever seen royalty, but she supposed they wouldn't be dressed so simply or be wandering about without an entourage. The stories she had heard from some of the menfolk seemed to indicate that whenever anyone of importance went on a journey, he took half the household with him to attend to his needs. She remembered that Elder Drao had once told of witnessing the arrival of a lord in one of the downmeadow villages. The whole township had turned out, decked in their best dress. The lord had dozens of servants with him, finery that could not be described. The feast he had shared with the village had been talked about for years after. Drao had described the foods and the entertainment over and over. The spectacle had grown grander with each retelling, until Vala had almost forgotten the original. She smiled now at the memory. Drao had been one of the few in the village with whom she had shared a friendship, but he was dead many seasons past. The only one left who cared at all what happened to her was Lawanda.

Vala's steps slowed, her memories rushing over her with cold finality. How could she go back to her village? How could she face Lawanda after what had happened to the baby? After what she had caused? She had prevented Lawanda's child from being accepted into the fae realm. She had condemned the child to an eternity without a soul. She couldn't go back. She just couldn't. Better to let Lawanda think she had died.

"Aric," she said quietly, stopping.

He stopped as well and turned to look at her. "What? What's wrong now?"

"I--I don't want to go back to my village."

"What?" Aric's voice squeaked with astonishment. "I thought you wanted to get out of fae land, get home to your own people."

"I--I do. I mean, I want out of the Faery Realm, but I don't want to go home."

"Then where do you want to go? I don't know your land. I don't know where other villages are. What am I supposed to do?"

She flinched at the anger in his voice. "You don't have to find me a village," she told him. "Just get me across the border, or whatever you call it. I can find a village on my own."

"Fine!" He spun around and strode away.

Vala followed, her heart pounding in trepidation. Find another village? Not likely. This was the first time she had ever been outside of Strander. She didn't have the slightest idea where to go. She would most likely wander about aimlessly, finally dying of hunger, if some wild animal didn't attack her first.

They crested a hill, and she caught her breath as a strong gust of wind grabbed at her. The sand swirled around her, stinging her skin. She narrowed her eyes, then reached up to shield them against the sand.

"Wonderful," Aric muttered, then trudged back down the hill. "The storm has hit."

Vala followed. "What are we going to do? Wait here until the storm passes?"

"No, unless you don't want to get home." He opened the pack and pulled out some bandaging cloth. He handed her a length, then tied one about his nose and mouth. "Do the same," he instructed.

When she had complied, he motioned once more to the top of the hill.

Vala sighed. "Can't we rest for a little while? Maybe the storm will be short-lived."

He didn't answer, just climbed the hill. Shoulders sagged in resignation, Vala again followed.

The wind's strength rapidly increased, picking up sand and flinging it sideways at her. The cloth kept it out of her nose and mouth, but her eyes were soon gritty and sore. Still Aric moved on, seemingly oblivious to her discomfort. Aric had said they would re-enter her world by nightfall. Now that they were so close, Vala wondered if that was what she truly wanted.

Chapter Six

Vala yelled out Aric's name again, and again her voice was swallowed by the howling winds. In despair, she sank to the ground, only to rise again for fear she would be buried alive by the blowing sands. She had somehow lost sight of Aric in the sandstorm. One moment he had been directly in front of her, the next he was gone. She wondered if he had planned it that way.

She shook her head, trying to dislodge the unwelcome thought, and trudged onward, although which direction she walked, she didn't know. Not that it mattered. If she didn't find Aric, she would surely die. He had the pack and all of the provisions. Without water she wouldn't last a day in the desert.

Besides that, her injured finger ached mercilessly. The swelling in her hand and wrist, red-hot and painful to the touch, indicated the infection had spread upward. Without help, she could well die of the infection as much as thirst.

"Aric!" she screamed again.

Only the howling winds answered.

She turned in a circle, walking backward, then gasped as she stumbled over something and fell. Her fingers touched a small bit of scrub, and she desperately began to search for more. She guessed she must have reached the border of the forest and the desert. Aric had been right. The route Severrani had taken had been circuitous.

More of the brush rose out of the sands to prick her hands, and she winced as pain flared up her arm. On hands and knees she crawled forward, her hopes soaring as more and more of the grass appeared.

Finally, the sands and howling winds stopped. Just like that. As if someone had closed a door on them. Vala looked back, stunned. The desert was gone. A great, cool, dark forest surrounded her, pressing against her from all sides. Relief replaced shock, and she realized she had crossed the border from Talede back onto the human side. It had been easy. Too easy. She couldn't begin to fathom how the fae kept people from tumbling into their lands on a regular basis.

She rose and took several tentative steps into the woods, then stopped to unwrap the cloth from her face and to shake the sand out of her hair and clothing. She wanted to call out for Aric, but somehow the quiet of the forest stopped any words. Not that it would do any good, she told herself. If he was still on the other side, he probably couldn't even hear her. She walked farther into the forest, hoping she would find water.

Those parts of her face that had been exposed to the stinging sands were red and raw. It hurt to even touch. She was grateful that Aric had shown her how to protect her mouth and nose, although her eyes burned and blurred. She stumbled more than once and, at last, collapsed, spent.

Her gaze turned skyward, though there was little evening sky visible through the thick forest canopy. Still, she saw the faint twinkle of a star and made a silent wish, her traitorous thoughts on Severrani. She hoped he was all right, that he had been able to take shelter from the storm. Tears washed the sand from her eyes, trickled down her cheeks and dripped from her chin. She had no place to go. She was truly adrift and alone for the first time in her young life. She had no supplies, no protection. The woods about her suddenly seemed ominous, and she crawled beneath the drooping branches of a large cedar tree to hide. Every sound, every sigh of tree limbs, every skittering of an animal, sent fear tearing through her. She wished she'd never left Severrani. She wished she'd never had to leave Strander. She wished she had never been saved by the Outsider. With a sob, she closed her eyes and cried herself to sleep.

She woke in pain, her hand and face throbbing and her throat so dry she could barely swallow. She remained still, listening, picking out the sounds about her, then crawled from her hiding spot. Her head reeled as she stood, and she gripped the cedar branches for support. Her gaze drifted in the direction of the desert that she could no longer see. The storm must be over by now, and Vala prayed for Aric's safety. Despite his gloomy and sarcastic personality, she worried about what might have happened to him.

She looked around. The forest must have ample water. It was so green, so alive. She began to walk, her joints stiff and sore, her head spinning. At length she heard more than the soft sigh of the wind through the treetops. From somewhere came the gurgle of water. Her heart raced with anticipation, but she forced herself to be calm, to search out the stream with logic, not desperation. Water flowed downhill. The land beneath her feet sloped to the right, most likely southeast. Drawing a deep breath, Vala began to walk that direction.

How long she walked was uncertain, but by the time she did spot the small stream she was almost too weak to reach it. She stumbled forward, fell to her knees and plunged her uninjured hand into the icy water, scooping it up to pour into her parched mouth and throat. Some dribbled down the front of her shirt, but it felt so refreshing she didn't care. She would have jumped in fully clothed if the stream had been bigger, but she satisfied herself with splashing the water all over her face and head, then bending over and swishing her hair in it as well.

Her scalp stung and smarted, and she realized that it, too, must have been scoured raw by the raging sands. She squeezed the water out of her hair, noticing that the ends were, indeed, now a white-blonde color. With a shrug, she tossed the wet strands over her shoulders, then pulled off her tattered shoes, and thrust her aching feet into the stream. The cold water was wonderful, running over her blistered skin, swirling about her thin ankles and soaking through her pant legs. She wanted nothing more than to stay here in the cool of the forest and rest.

A sudden wry chuckle escaped her. Why shouldn't she? She had no pressing place to be, no one to answer to. There was no one about but her. Keeping her feet in the water, she lay back on the riverbank and stared skyward. She caught a brief glimpse of the early morning sky, visible through the treetops as they swayed in the wind. An incredible sense of peace washed over her, and not even her throbbing hand could detract from it. In fact, it was too peaceful. A frown furrowed her brow.

The boundaries of Larandalath hadn't been that far away from where she, Aric and Severanni had made camp. She had seen the shimmering colors of the land beyond the desert to the east. Aric had taken her southeast, claiming it was a faster way to her own home. But what if he had been wrong? What if she had become confused in the storm? What if she had entered that enchanted forest she had seen from atop the sandy hill? What if, in her confusion, she had actually entered Larandalath?

Vala sat up so quickly her head spun. Her gaze swept the forest about her. It didn't look like anything special, nothing spectacular, no color that seemed more vibrant or stronger than any other. Yet, how would she know? She had never even been in a real forest until Severrani had taken her there.

The meadow! She would know by the colors in the meadow. She grabbed her shoes, jerked her feet from the water and hurriedly dressed. She tried to determine her direction from the bit of sky she could see. She had never been good with direction. She hadn't needed to be. She had never gone anywhere unaccompanied. Except once, and she wasn't going to think about that right now.

She started forward, not at all sure just where she was headed. She hadn't gone far when voices reached her. Familiar voices. Heart pounding, she moved ahead more cautiously, then stopped, startled.

"I don't know where she is!" Aric cried, his voice holding a touch of panic. "I think she was trying to get back to her own world."

"You *think*?" Severrani's voice was cold and angry.

Vala peered through the trees, but she could see neither of the fae. They sounded quite close. She waited for either of them to speak again, trying to pinpoint their position.

"What difference does it make, anyway?" Aric asked. "She wanted to go home."

"She cannot," Severrani retorted.

Vala almost spoke up, demanding to know why she couldn't. Instead, she backed away from the voices as Aric asked her question for her.

"Why not?" Aric asked. "Why is it so important that she be delivered to my father? It's not as if she could do anything to help me. He's going to punish me if she's there or not. Besides, he has enough women around him now. He certainly doesn't need another one."

There was a momentary pause before Severrani answered, and even then his explanation sounded forced and unnatural, as if he were merely reciting words with little meaning. "The Law states that any human entering our world is to go before the king. You know that, or at least you should."

"Why should I? It's not as if I'll ever be king. I have no claims to the throne. I'm just a bastard child, after all." The words were spoken with bitterness and grief.

"Your father's indiscretions are not your burden, Aric," Severrani replied.

Vala lifted her eyebrows in surprise at the gentle tone of concern and reassurance in the words. The fae continually surprised her with his words and actions. She glanced at her injured finger, which still throbbed mercilessly. He had only been trying to help her. Just as the Outsider had tried to help her and her people. The Outsider's reward had been banishment, perhaps even death after his beating. And her payment to Severrani? Guilt rushed through her, but it was not enough to make her step forward and announce her presence.

What did it matter? She was nothing to him. She was to be delivered to the king and that was that. Resignation firmed her resolve, and she crept away.

She walked the remainder of the day, her heart heavy with sadness. She had stayed close to the little stream, following it downhill, but had found nothing she knew to be edible. At least she had cold water to drink, but by nightfall, her stomach was rumbling, her head reeled and she could barely manage to lift her feet from the ground. Finally, she sagged onto a fallen tree, exhausted.

The woods were cold and dark. Strange rustling noises came from the gloom about her, sending chills racing along her arms and up her neck. She shivered, crossed her arms over her chest, and pulled her shawl closer. It did little to warm her physically, but the mere presence brought her comfort. She pulled on the cord about her neck, drawing out the medallion for the first time in days. She had almost forgotten about, she had been so immersed in just surviving her ordeal. Now, it offered her a familiar comfort.

The moonlight that managed to break through the treetops caressed the medallion gently. Vala ran her fingers over the etched words once again. *Elthea Gannabribriel, Ithys Kjvali.* Had the Outsider been fae, or had the fae given him the medallion? She didn't think the latter was likely. After all, why would the fae give something that seemed so valuable to another? Yet, the Outsider had given it to her mother. It didn't make sense. Even as sheltered as Vala was, she knew value when she saw it. Too many questions rattled her tired mind, and she slid from the tree to the ground to sleep.

She woke much later to a light drizzle and strangely familiar sounds. It took her a few moments to identify them, but finally she realized that she was listening to the *thwack-thwack* of a blade striking wood. She rose unsteadily, tied the shawl about her head, then followed the sound. Not far away, a half-dozen men were felling trees and splitting them for fuel. Vala involuntarily gasped as a sizable tree plummeted to the earth, crashing through the foliage and bringing down several smaller trees in its fall. She felt the trees' death like a knife through her heart. Unexpected anger assailed her, and before she could stop herself she rushed forward.

"Stop it!" she shrieked. "Leave the trees alone! Stop!"

The six men fell back with a collective gasp of surprise, followed by fear and wonder. They clustered together, axes held in limp hands, eyes focused on her, as the branches of the trees about them calmed and quieted. Vala looked at the fallen tree.

"How could you?" she whispered, her heart suddenly overwhelmed with grief.

"We--we seek wood to keep our fires burning through the winter," one of the men managed.

Vala turned to look at him, wondering not only at her unexpected emotions but also at the fear that now lay on the men's faces. Recognition slowly dawned. She knew these men. They were of her village. But they seemed different somehow. Older.

"Lel?" she breathed. "Hanlick?"

The two men she had identified exchanged startled glances.

"You know us?" Lel asked, his voice a coarse whisper.

"Yes," Vala returned. "And you know me. I am Vala. I live in your village, with Tyrs and Lawanda."

There was a heavy silence before Hanlick moved cautiously forward. He studied Vala through narrowed eyes, then rubbed his grizzled chin.

"We thought you were dead," he murmured.

"You've been gone a long time," Lel added.

Vala frowned. "No, not really. Just a few days." She took a step backward, overwhelmed with a sudden urge to run.

"No!" Hanlick cried, "Don't go."

Vala's unease increased, and she took another step back.

"You don't look well, Vala," Lel said.

Her gaze moved to her hand, red and swollen beneath the bandage. "I-- I'm not," she admitted. She reached out to steady herself on a nearby tree.

It was all the distraction the men needed. They moved forward in a rush, seizing her before she could move. Hanlick twisted her arms behind her back, sending agony tearing through her.

"Get the ropes!" he ordered the other men. "We caught ourselves a fae!"

"No!" Vala screamed and struggled vainly against the strong hold they had on her. But she was no match for their size or strength, and Hanlick figured out soon enough that putting pressure on her injured hand nearly dropped her in a faint.

The men tied her hands securely behind her back, then tied her ankles as well. Hanlick picked her up and threw her into the back of the wood cart as if she were nothing more than cargo, and the men piled in around her. Lel leapt to the bench, picked up the reins and set the horses in frantic motion.

"Please," Vala begged. "It's as I told you! I am Vala, from your own village. Ask Lawanda! Fetch her. She'll tell you!"

But the men weren't listening.

"Does she have magic?" one of the younger men whispered.

Vala seized the fear. "Yes!" she shrieked. Tears of agony blurred her vision, anger her senses. "You will bring the wrath of the fae down upon yourselves unless you let me go!"

Bern, one of the younger men, scooted back, his dark eyes holding fear, but the older men seemed merely nonplussed. Vala struggled again against her restraints, grimacing as the ropes cut into her infected hand. Finally, she lay still, eyes closed against the nightmare around her.

Everything would be all right, she told herself. Lawanda would recognize her and stop this insanity. She would be released. She took deep, calming breaths, willing her heart to stop racing, her stomach to stop churning. Everything would be all right.

It took them the better part of the morning to return to the village. During that time, none of the men spoke with her or offered her anything to eat or drink. By the time the wagon rolled into the tiny village she was exhausted and sick.

Villagers came to greet the men, obviously surprised by their early return. When they saw Vala trussed up in the back of the wagon, they fell back with alarmed cries. Lel brought the wagon to a stop outside the church, where Hanlick and the others leapt to the ground.

"Revered!" someone cried. "Revered! You must come at once!"

Vala twisted her head, recognizing the call for the church elder. Her heart sank. He had shown no great love for her during her years in Strander. He would as soon condemn her as look at her.

"What is it?" he called, approaching. "What do you have?"

He stopped with a gasp before the wagon. His dark eyes went wide and he looked at Hanlick in question.

"We found her in the forest," Hanlick said. "She saw us, condemned us for cutting wood for the village. She claims she is Vala, the wench that disappeared from here some months back."

Vala sucked in her breath. "Months?" she cried. "No! It--it was only a few days ago!" Her panic increased as her gaze took in the villagers gathered around her. Alarm tore through her as her uncle approached, leaning heavily on his cane. His face was set in a hard scowl; his eyes narrowed with hate.

"She returns!" he spat. "As I feared. She returns to gloat over the evils of her kind!" He shook his cane at her. "She used her vile magic on me. Nearly killed me!" He turned toward the assembled villagers. "And she will use her magic on you, every one of you, unless we do something about it!"

The villagers shrank back, murmuring amongst themselves, their faces registering true fear. The Revered stepped forward, removed the church medallion from his neck and placed it around Vala's.

"You may untie her feet now," he instructed the men.

Lel did as told, though Vala could see the wariness in his eyes. Once freed of the ankle bonds, Vala struggled to sit up.

"Where is Lawanda?" she cried. "And Tyrs? They'll know me."

The Revered studied her through narrowed eyes, then reached out and pulled her shawl from her head. Her white hair tumbled out, drawing a gasp from the people. For a moment, no one spoke, then the Revered motioned for Bern to summon Tyrs.

"Tyrs!" Bern bellowed, his voice echoing in the village square.

Vala scanned the crowd, finally picking out the young man. He stumbled forward, his face pale, lined with grief. He stopped before her.

"Tyrs!" she sobbed. "You know me! Please, tell them who I am. Please!"

He was quiet, his gaze riveted on her, on her eyes, her hair, the medallion that lay on her chest. Tears pooled in his dark eyes. "Why?" he rasped. "Why have you returned? Is it not enough that you took my children? Now you have taken my own wife."

Vala stared at him. "Lawanda?" she breathed, then louder as horror gripped her. "Lawanda! Where is she? Let me go!" She struggled fiercely against her bonds, ignoring the pain that blazed through her hand, that left her shaking and weak.

The villagers let out muffled shrieks of terror and hastily retreated. The Revered held up his bony hands.

"Enough, demon!" he ordered. "You should know that Lawanda is no longer with us. When you left with her child she sought you out, to ask--nay, beg--you to return the infant to its proper place. Instead, you took her body and soul as well."

"No!" Vala screamed. "I am not fae! I didn't take anyone! Lawanda!" She struggled to her feet, peering over the villagers' heads, trying to spot her friend. "Lawanda!"

Hanlick made a grab for her ankles, toppling her back to the hard wood of the wagon. Her head slammed against the bench in the front as she fell. For a moment spots danced before her eyes, then, with a sob, she fell into darkness.

Chapter Seven

Vala stared at the wooden walls surrounding her. Or what she could see of them. Moonlight pressed against the slats, creeping into the small, wooden shed where Vala had been imprisoned. The villagers had left her with nothing save the dirt floor and whatever vermin scurried about in the dark. The shed had been emptied of the tools once stored there. There was only a half empty sack of grain, which the rats had obviously feasted on.

She shifted her position, again worrying the knots of rope that bound her wrists, though the action sent pain searing through her hand and arm. The Revered's medallion thudded against the medallion hidden beneath her shirt, and she looked down at it. What had the Revered hoped to gain by hanging his religious emblem about her neck? That it would prevent her use of the magic she was supposed to hold? That she would be docile and limp under its influence? The mere thought sickened her, and she twisted about, trying to work the heavy cord over her head. But it was to no avail, and at last she gave up, sagging back against the wall of the shed.

Her hand ached, each beat of her heart pulsing pain through it. She wished now for Severrani's gentle touch, his medicine that would take the agony away. Tears threatened, as they had so often since she had wakened in this dark place. Why had she ever thought she could return? And what was all of this talk about her being gone for several months?

They had told her nothing. They hadn't even brought her food or water, and now she was weak and dizzy. The fact that these people knew her, admitted to it, yet still believed her to be fae shattered her heart. And Odig-- the mere thought of the demented old man, sent shudders through her. She prayed that he would not be allowed to get near her.

She leaned her head back and stared upward at the moon through a crack in the roof. Her thoughts drifted to Severrani. She wondered where he had gone, what had happened to Aric, if the boy had returned to his father, and how his father had reacted to the mistake in the meadows.

The meadows reminded her of Lawanda, and once again grief brought a lump to her throat. What had Lawanda done? Where had she gone? Vala had not even considered that the woman would try to follow her. What had happened to her?

Months. The idea seemed preposterous. How could the villagers be telling her what she knew couldn't be true? She hadn't been gone more than a few days, a week at the most. Still, from what she had seen of the village, it did look different, and the people looked different somehow as well. She shook her head, sighed and fell into troubled sleep, her head throbbing in time with her heartbeat.

Hanlick awakened her next morning. He pounded on the wooden side of the shed to gain her attention, and, when he had it, he said, "You'll be taken before the Council this morning. They will decide your fate."

Vala sagged in despair, not even wanting to speculate on what that might be. "Can I have some water?" she asked quietly.

"Water?" Hanlick seemed truly surprised by the request.

"Yes, I'm thirsty and hungry as well."

"I didn't realize fae ate or drank," Hanlick muttered, then nodded. "I shall get you something to eat and drink."

Vala watched him leave, cringing at the sound of the heavy crossbar being lowered against the outside of the door. As if she could escape the ropes and chains that bound her to the shed wall. The thought was almost laughable. Here she was, no bigger than a child, and restrained as if she were a bear.

Hanlick returned just moments later with a tray of food--bread, honey and tea. He set it down just within her reach, then hurriedly backed away. Vala looked up at him through eyes foggy with fever.

"My hand is infected," she said. "I had some herbs in my room at Lawanda's house. Could you fetch them? Please?"

He paused, a frown furrowing his brow. "Your room?" Hanlick regarded her through narrowed eyes. "Tyrs destroyed everything in that room shortly after you left."

Vala gasped. "All of my things? My trunk, my parent's--"

"They were burned."

Vala stared at him in shock. "Burned?"

"No one wanted anything to do with a demon here." He paused, rubbing at his chin. "I have to say, you don't like a demon."

"Because I am not!" Vala cried, then softened her voice as he cringed. "Can I at least have my shawl?"

Again he hesitated. "I will ask the Revered," he finally said and left, again bolting the door.

"Wait!" Vala called, but it was too late. She stared at the meager breakfast offerings. Hanlick had not unchained her hands. Not that it mattered. She was too sick at heart to eat, anyway, her appetite stalled by the devastating news. All of her things - burned. All that she treasured, gone. It was as if she never existed. Tears stung her eyes, but she refused to let them flow. If she started crying now, she might never stop. She sat back to wait her time before the council.

It came sooner than she was prepared for. Hanlick and Bern arrived to escort her to the church, which also served as a meeting hall. She blinked in the mid-morning sunshine as she was led from the shed into the dusty streets. While Hanlick near dragged her, Bern's touch was gentler, the look on his face one of resignation more than fear. She wondered if she might have an ally in the young man.

The villagers gathered in the church to watch as she was marched down the center of the church, her chains rattling. She realized what a sight she must make--dirty, mussed, wearing clothing too big for her. It was no wonder the villagers shrank back from her. That, and the fact that her hair, almost completely white, was knotted and tangled, and dotted with bits of dirt, grass and leaves. She found it ironic that she was now allowed inside the church when she had not been so for many years.

The Revered stood at the pulpit wearing the black robes of his trade. Several religious emblems hung about his neck, as if he thought to ward off her evil with them. It almost made her laugh with the ridiculousness of it all. Almost. But her terror was too great, and she sobbed as she was pushed to the floor before the pulpit.

"You have been brought before the Council to answer to charges," the holy man stated, his voice booming in the small church.

"What charges?" Vala asked, looking up at him.

"You have caused this village much heartache in the past nineteen years, demon! Because of you, the children have died-- "

"No!" Vala cried, trying to stand. "I have --"

"Silence!" the Revered ordered. "We thought we were rid of you once. Now, this Council has decided that we must rid ourselves of your evil for eternity. You have hereby been condemned to death, demon!"

Vala sagged to her knees, stunned. "Death?"

"Prayer will do you no good now," the Revered said. "It has been decided. So shall it be. Execution will take place tomorrow in the village square. Death by fire."

Vala stared at him, too horrified to speak. She heard Bern gasp, and glanced his way. His face was pale, his mouth gaping in shock. He watched as Hanlick pulled her to her feet and dragged her back down the aisle. She caught Tyrs' gaze briefly, silently pleading with him for help, but he merely averted his gaze, and she was returned her to the confines of the shed.

"Hanlick," she begged. "Please, don't do this. You know me. I haven't done anything wrong. Please!"

Hanlick grunted in dismissal, and shut and locked the door. Vala stared into the cool dimness of the shed, then abruptly turned and retched into the dirt. How could they do this to her? How could they accuse her of causing all of the deaths for the past nineteen years? How could they call her a demon? She leaned her head against the wooden wall, finally allowing her tears to surface. She cried for not just what was happening now, but for everything she had endured in her short life. She cried for her lonely childhood, for her deceased parents, for her lost friends. She cried for Severrani, for the times she had hurt him. She cried for Aric, guessing what sort of life he must have with his father. And she cried for herself, for the aching emptiness of her heart and soul. At last, she fell into tortured sleep, her nightmares those of fire and then darkness.

She woke to night and a raging fever. The infection had spread up her arm, making every movement agony. Not that it mattered. By this time tomorrow she would be dead, consumed in the flames of ignorance.

She stiffened at the sound of a noise outside the shed. Her pulse quickened, and she strained her eyes through the darkness, waiting for the shed door to open. The sound of the bar being moved was barely audible, and a moment later, the door opened a mere slit. Vala waited, her breath coming in short, frightened gasps. The moonlight silhouetted a man's figure as he slipped into the shed. Vala twisted her hands in a desperate attempt to escape her bonds, tears of pain blurring her sight. Images of her uncle, of his heavy cane flashed through her mind. She would not endure any more of his blows, any more of his touches. And just as swiftly as she banished those thoughts, she remembered her rape. Her panic increased, and a scream lodged in a throat too constricted with terror to allow its escape.

The man approached, and Vala's breath hissed from her with relief as a beam of moonlight shone down on Tyrs' face.

"Tyrs," she breathed, her voice on the verge of hysteria. "You believe me, don't you? You won't let them do this to me. Please, help me. Please."

He hunkered down before her. "If I help you escape," he said quietly, "will you return Lawanda to me?"

"What?" Vala stared at him in confusion.

"Will you return to your land and bring Lawanda back to me?" he pressed.

Vala didn't know what to say. How could she promise something she couldn't deliver? Yet, if she rejected this one chance at freedom she knew her fate. She licked dry lips and nodded.

"I will. I promise," she whispered. "Please, Tyrs, just release me. Please."

He paused for a moment, his gaze darting furtively back at the open door. Then he quickly reached behind her and loosed the ropes and chains.

Vala drew her arms forward, rubbing at the raw skin on her wrists, wincing at the pain of her infection. Tyrs backed away, his face wary, as Vala got slowly to her feet. Her head reeled, and she held to the wall for support.

"I need some water, Tyrs," she murmured.

"I don't have any," he replied.

Vala's gaze went to the cold meal Hanlick had brought earlier. She bent and snatched up the cup, spilling half the contents before she could drink the rest. She clutched the small chunk of bread in a dirty hand and looked toward Tyrs.

He backed away another step, as if he thought she would pounce on him. "If you're going to go, then go. Quickly. But remember your promise, Vala. If you fail me, I swear I will come seeking you myself."

The hard tone of his voice cut into her heart, and she pushed away from the wall, moving slowly toward the door. Tyrs stepped out of her way. With a last look at him, she slipped outside, then slid along the side of the shed and into the darkness beyond.

When she was safely away from the village, she broke into a staggering run, panic giving her strength. The cold night air stung her cheeks, turned her tears to icy streaks, left her throat raw. Still, she ran. Sounds crept out of the night to torment her, driving her first one way, then the other. Fear swelled up in her chest, choking her, stealing her breath from her lungs. She was once again being pursued through darkness, only this time her tormentors were invisible.

Finally, she fell and lay gasping, sprawled in the fragrant flowers of the Funeral Meadow. She had not even realized that her flight was taking her there. She rolled onto her back to stare into the dark sky, her chest heaving, her stomach threatening to send up the tea. Somewhere in her run she had dropped the bread, but she no longer cared. She was free, that was all that mattered now. The air was chill, the breeze stiff, and Vala shivered as she slowly sat up. The two medallions clanked together and Vala tore the religious emblem from her neck, repulsed by the reason it had been placed there.

Stealthy sounds rustled through the grasses, and Vala twisted her head, trying to make out the source. Dark shadows flitted at the edge of the meadow, and terror gripped Vala. Wolves!

She got slowly to her feet, her breath coming in short, ragged gasps. Cautiously, she began to back away, seeking the shelter of the rocks to her right. The shadows moved to cut her off, and she froze, searching desperately for some other place to hide.

Slender trees swayed in the breeze, their leafy branches dark against the night sky. They would be too weak to hold even her slight weight. Despair brought a lump to her throat, and she turned toward the village. Where else could she go? She didn't think the wolves would follow her to a human settlement. *Human? Where had that thought come from?* She grimaced. A low growl moved through the meadows, and Vala's terror turned to pure panic.

Without thinking, she broke into a run, racing away from the meadow and the shadows that stalked her. She heard a rush of movement through the grasses, and a moment later, something wickedly sharp gripped her ankle. She flew forward, trying to stop her fall with her hands and failing. Black, furred bodies were upon her at once, teeth sinking into her flesh. She screamed in agony, trying to knock them away, but they grabbed at her flailing arms, their low growls becoming wild and excited as the scent of blood filled the air.

"Help!" Vala shrieked, her voice echoing over the dark lands. "Severrani! Aric! Someone, please help!"

One of the animals lunged forward and closed its sharp teeth over her throat. Vala felt the fangs puncture skin, and a muffled sob escaped her as she pushed against the beast with all of her waning strength. Her gaze met that of the animal and words came unbidden to her lips. "Ithys Gannabrina," she shrieked.

Red light shot out from the medallion, engulfing her. The wolves yelped, leaping away from her, then scattered with high-pitched keening. Vala struggled to sit up but could not. A powerful force flattened her against the ground, the spun her into darkness.

She opened her eyes to bright, early-morning sunshine. She lay still, staring into a sky of azure. Puffy white clouds floated lazily on a warm breeze that brought the scent of the sea. Vala opened and closed her hand, feeling sand beneath her fingers. Slowly, she turned her head. A sparkling white beach stretched as far as she could see. She turned to look the other direction, meeting with the same image. Was she back? Back in the land of the fae? Or was this the afterlife? Heaven?

Carefully, she sat up, not at all surprised to find that she bore no evidence of the wolves' attack. Even her infected hand was now healed, and she flexed it thankfully. The call of gulls high overhead drew her attention, and she watched them soar effortlessly over the blue-green waters. Waves washed up on the shore with a quiet shushing sound. Vala drew a deep breath of the clean air and closed her eyes in bliss.

So, this was what heaven was like. But shouldn't her family have met her? Her mother and father? She had always heard how loved ones met the newly deceased on the other side, guided them, comforted them. She opened her eyes and scanned her surroundings. Behind her loomed a great white cliff that sparkled as if it were made of millions of small jewels instead of dirt and rock. It reminded her of the white cliff she had tumbled over after leaving Strander. The border between her world and the world of the fae. A frown crossed her face, and she got to her feet. Could this place be nothing more? Was she again hovering between two worlds, neither of which she could claim as her own? With a sigh, she crossed the sands to look straight up the cliff.

Upon closer inspection she saw that small steps had been carved into the white rock. They wound upward, leaning into the cliff's face, until they disappeared at the top. Vala hesitated a moment, then began to climb.

The wind drifted past her, coiling around her body, lifting loose bits of clothing, playing gently in her white hair. She stopped, staring down at her clothing, at her hair that touched gently at her shoulders. She was clean, her hair no longer tangled and filled with plant matter. She ran her fingers through it, from scalp to tips, puzzled. No tangles met her searching fingertips. Her hair was soft, silky, and pure white. Puzzled, she turned back to the steps.

She had never done such climbing in her own world, and thought back to the rock tumble she had climbed with Severrani and Aric. She had been unskilled, fearful, clumsy. But now, here, she seemed to be able to climb with the grace of a mountain goat. There was absolutely no fear in her as she looked down at the sandy beach far below. She possessed an inner knowledge that told her she would not fall.

A small smile of satisfaction touched her lips as she reached the top of the cliff. She had done it. Behind her, the ocean stretched for an eternity, sparkling in the sunshine, while before her stretched a vast, rolling prairie of golden grasses. The wind ruffled the grain, making it appear as if the entire land undulated, rising and cresting and falling, much as the waves on the sea at her back.

Vala filled her lungs with the fresh air, then lifted her arms to the sky. She felt more alive than she ever had, free, at one with the land that surrounded her. Surely this was indeed heaven. A movement to her right caught her attention.

"Mama?" she called. "Papa?" She walked along the edge of the cliff, eyes narrowed in curiosity, then stopped with a gasp of surprise.

A small, shaggy pony stood amongst the grain, chewing on its bit. It eyed Vala with calm acceptance, then shook its equally shaggy head. She went toward it, hand held before her.

"Hello, sweet thing," she whispered. "What are you doing way out here, all alone?" She ran one hand along its pudgy cheek.

The animal shuddered from head to tail, then nickered softly. Vala smiled and glanced about the fields.

"Well, it's obvious someone brought you here," she murmured. "I wonder who?"

An excited little giggle came from the grass, and Vala turned toward the sound. She was amazed at how calm she felt. It was as if all of the terror of the past few days belonged to someone else, in another world. She smiled. She had no reservations about speaking, about being seen.

"Well, come, then, show yourself."

There was a moment of silence, then two children, a boy and a girl no more than eight years of age, stood up. Their hair glowed golden, almost blending in with the wheat. Their brown eyes were wide, set in cherubic faces with apple-red cheeks. They held to each other's hands and looked at Vala in open wonder and awe.

"My name is Vala," she said softly, wondering if two small angels stood before her.

They giggled, looking at each other, before looking back at her.

"Are you a faery?" the boy asked in a voice so soft and sweet Vala almost didn't hear the question.

She hesitated, and the little girl poked him in the ribs with her elbow.

"I don't think you're supposed to ask them that," she whispered. "You'll make her disappear."

The little boy looked at Vala, aghast.

"A faery?" she asked, suddenly wary. She glanced about, but she was alone with the two children.

After a moment's hesitation, the little girl spoke up. "Mama says that lots of faeries used to live here, but they are all gone now."

"Really?" Vala looked at her thoughtfully. "Where did they go?"

"Don't you know?" the little girl asked.

Vala paused, then sighed. "No, I'm new here. This isn't my land." She didn't think she should tell them she wasn't a faery. So far, they had seemed very accepting of her.

The little boy squinted up at her. "Some people say the faeries went across the water, there." He pointed toward the sea. "And some say that they died of broken hearts when the first people came here and ruined their beautiful lands. Papa says that the first people were not very nice, not like us. They came here and cut down lots of trees, took the wood without asking the faeries first. They ruined some of the lakes and rivers, too. And they dug into the hills looking for gold."

"I see," Vala murmured. "I suppose that could make the faeries leave."

"How come you're here?" the little girl asked. "Are the faeries coming back?"

"Back?" Vala sighed again, confused. "I am not sure where I am to be honest. What is this place called?"

The children giggled, but the boy answered. "Gannabrina. Where else?"

Vala sucked in her breath. Gannabrina? Had she not spoken that word in the Funeral Meadow? Just as the wolves were at her throat? Her hand went to her chest, and closed on the medallion. She remembered now, remembered the red light, the spinning sensation, the force that had pressed her into the ground. She started when the little boy suddenly spoke.

"My name is Vaedon," he said. "This is my sister, Aerawin. Will you come to our house and meet our parents?"

At that, Vala balked, old fears returning. Just because the children here were so accepting, didn't mean their parents would be.

"It's not far to our house," Aerawin said. "You can ride on Prea if you would like."

Vala looked at the small, shaggy horse with a sudden smile. "No, I don't think that's a good idea. I can walk beside you." She winced, realizing she'd just agreed to go with the two children. A sudden thought occurred to her. "Do either of you know a place called Gannabribriel or Elthea?"

They shook their heads, golden locks shimmering in the sunshine. Vaedon's eyes glowed with pride. "But I'll bet my papa knows. He knows just about everything about Gannabrina."

"Very well, I'll go with you." Vala reached out to help them astride the horse, but they both shied away from her hands. She drew back, unsure and suddenly on guard.

"What's wrong?" she asked softly.

The little boy went red. "I--I don't want to hurt you!" he blurted. "Mama says that touching a faery would hurt them, maybe even kill them."

"Oh." Vala whispered, then sighed. "Well, touching me won't hurt. Not as long as the touch is done with love and acceptance. I promise. See?" She held out both hands toward them.

The children looked at each other, then back at Vala. Hesitantly, the little boy reached out. When his small fingers finally touched hers it sent a tingle shooting through her. She caught her breath in surprise. It was as if her mind had connected with his, as if she knew his innermost desires and wishes. He was a gentle soul, a compassionate boy, filled with love and warmth.

Vala held out her other hand to the little girl, who grinned and slipped her small hand into Vala's. Again, Vala felt the strange tingling, reaching to her very soul, telling her what her usual senses could not. These children would not lead her into harm, of that she was sure. The gentleness of their spirits filled her heart. She lifted them one by one onto the back of the horse.

Vaedon took up the reins, while Aerawin held tight to his waist. Seated, the children were now eye-level with Vala, and Aerawin reached out hesitantly to touch Vala's hair.

"Your hair is so pretty," she murmured. "And so soft."

For some reason, the words reminded Vala of her mother's shawl, lost now in the village that had disowned her. "My mother used to make shawls and blankets that were as soft," she told Aerawin. "I lost the only one that I had."

Aerawin frowned with empathy. "Perhaps my mama can give you one of hers. She spins yarn from angora goats."

"Angora? I have never heard of those, but I should like to see one."

They grinned at her and Vaedon nudged the horse into motion. Vala walked alongside, trepidation slowing her steps. What if the children's parents reacted with fear and loathing of her? What if they tried to imprison her as well? She reached up to grip the medallion about her neck. Wearing a pendant that held such words as this one could be very good or it could be very bad. She couldn't imagine that the word Gannabribriel being so nearly the same as this place was a coincidence, and she wondered if this was the land across the water that Severrani had spoken of. The land, thoughts of which, had brought such yearning and loneliness to his voice, yet had caused him to turn aside in anger and resignation. Vala wondered why. Well, perhaps this visit with the children's parents would prove enlightening. She only hoped it didn't prove deadly.

It didn't take them long to reach the crest of a hill, where they paused. Vaedon pointed to a cottage nestled against the backdrop of a copse of aspen. Smoke curled from the stone chimney, carried away on the gentle breeze that stirred the wheat and set the aspen leaves to quaking. The leaves looked like small jewels as the sunlight caught them, reflecting off their green, silver and orange surfaces. The white trunks glowed as if they possessed an inner light, and again Vala was seized with a sense of peace and belonging.

"That's home," Vaedon said, and his words rang true in Vala's heart. "See, there's the barn for the animals. We don't have many. Just a few horses and the goats."

"Then a village must be close by," Vala said, her worry returning. If she had to deal only with the children's parents, she might be able to run and hide. But if a whole village came after her, she would have no defense. She clutched the medallion tighter.

Vaedon nodded. "It's not far. About a half-day's ride in the wagon. Come on, it's almost lunch time." He urged the pony down the rise, and Vala followed.

Two yapping dogs raced out to meet them, tails wagging and tongues lolling. The animals leapt about Vala's legs, their eyes bright with curiosity and happiness. She smiled and reached out to pet the nearest one, a large, golden-coated animal. It stood on its hind legs, put its paws on her arm and licked her neck with a long, sloppy tongue. Vala drew back with a gasp, her memory of the wolves still strong in her mind. Only through willpower did she force herself to relax and accept the animal's greeting, knowing it meant no harm.

The other dog, a smaller black, shaggy beast, ran about Vala's ankles, licking her legs. The children laughed with delight and slipped from the pony's back. Vala glanced up as a woman stepped from the house, no doubt drawn by the dogs' barking. She shielded her eyes against the sun to peer in the children's direction. Even from this distance, Vala could plainly see her face.

The woman appeared at first puzzled, then her eyes grew wide and her mouth formed a small circle of astonishment. She hurriedly brushed stray locks of hair into place and smoothed her apron and skirts as if she stood before royalty. The children nearly dragged Vala toward their mother, their excitement evident.

"Mama, look!" Vaedon cried. "It's a faery. Her name is Vala, and she's really nice."

The woman swallowed hard, her gaze flying to the hold the children maintained on Vala's hands. "You--you're touching her," she whispered. "You mustn't."

"No, Mama," Aerawin declared. "She said it was all right. It doesn't hurt her at all." She looked up at Vala, pure adoration in her eyes. "This is my mama. Her name is Elaewen. My papa's name is Frayhan. He's out in the fields, but he'll be coming in soon for lunch. Then you'll get to meet him, too."

Elaewen looked at Vala with open reverence. "We welcome you, M'lady. Please accept our humble home as yours." She motioned to the doorway. "Are you hungry? Thirsty? Would you like to rest?"

Vala was momentarily too stunned to answer. She was amazed at the difference in the response she was getting from this woman and her children, and the way she had been treated in her own village. She nodded slowly, her heart filled with both relief and sadness.

"Actually, I am quite hungry and thirsty," she admitted, "but I do not wish to beg food and drink without payment of some kind."

"Your presence is all of the payment we need," Elaewen replied. "For, surely, our house has been blessed by your arrival. Please, come in." She led the way inside.

Vala, the children and the dogs followed. Elaewen turned at once to the animals.

"Oh, shoo! You needn't bring your filth and hair inside. Go!" She waved her hands at the animals, and they darted outside, barking wildly. Elaewen glanced out the doorway. "Here comes Papa. Vaedon, you'd best see to Prea before you eat. Aerawin, you need to feed the dogs. Please, Vala, sit down."

Vala did as requested, settling on the wooden bench at a small table as the children ran to obey their mother's instructions.

"Would you like water? Tea? Perhaps some mead?" Elaewen asked.

"Water would be fine," Vala replied, feeling a little uncomfortable at being waited on.

Elaewen drew her a cup from the pump at the sink and placed it before her with a smile. Vala took a long drink, savoring the icy liquid. Though it was refreshing, it didn't have the same light flavor that the water in Severrani's waterskin had held, and Vala's sigh escaped her before she could stop it. Elaewen's face crumpled into a worried frown at once.

"Could I get you something else?" she asked. "The water is from a well. Perhaps it is --"

"Oh, no!" Vala cried, "The water is wonderful. It--it just reminded me of something else, that's all."

Elaewen's face relaxed. "Oh, I see." She paused, then looked over as her husband entered the house.

He stopped short, his face registering surprise. "The children said... I--I just didn't believe it. Welcome, welcome to our home, M'lady." He bowed his head in Vala's direction.

She flushed and rose from the table. "Thank you. Thank you both for allowing me into your home. I--I can't tell you how much this means to me."

"We are the ones who are honored, M'lady," Frayhan said.

"M'lady?" Vala smiled. "No, it's just Vala. Please."

Frayhan reddened but nodded, then gestured toward the table again. "Please, sit. Elaewen is one of the best cooks in the land."

Elaewen smiled and turned back to the kitchen. "My husband speaks as one who is always hungry. To him, most anything considered food would be delicious."

Vala laughed and sat back down at the table, just as the children returned. A soft cry came from a room beyond the great room, and Vala glanced that direction.

"A baby?" she murmured.

"Yes." Frayhan smiled. "Vaedon, fetch your sister, will you?"

The little boy hurried into the other room and returned shortly, carrying a child of no more than three months. The little girl's copper locks curled about a face as clear and pure as porcelain. Large, blue eyes appraised Vala with curiosity before a smile puckered the red lips. Vala covered her mouth, stifling a gasp. The child was almost identical in coloring to Lawanda's baby.

Elaewen came toward Vala, her face concerned. She took the baby from Vaedon.

"Is there something wrong, M'lady?" she asked.

"N--no," Vala stammered. "She...it's just that..." She drew a deep, calming breath, though tears stung her eyes. "Your baby--she looks so much like a child my dearest friend just lost."

"Lost?" Frayhan repeated. "She died, then?" He cast a questioning glance at his wife. "Fae children are dying?"

Vala stared at him, unsure how to answer, her thoughts numb with renewed grief. Her gaze swept over the house, the family standing before her. An aching emptiness swelled inside her chest, threatened to overtake her. Tears trickled down her cheeks. This was the life she yearned for--to be part of a loving family, to live in a place of beauty and peace. She wanted her parents back, she wanted her youth back, she wanted things to be the way they had never been. She came to her feet, suddenly just wanting to escape, to tear herself away from such peace and tranquility. It tore at her heart, left her empty and yearning for something she could never have.

"I--I have to go," she muttered, moving toward the door.

"What's wrong, Faery?" Aerawin cried, clutching her hand. "Don't cry. You can stay here. We won't hurt you."

"Yes, please stay, Faery," Vaedon pleaded, taking her other hand. "We love you."

Vala stared at them, then suddenly sagged to her knees. She covered her face with her hands and sobbed into them. A moment later, she felt Elaewen's hands on hers, gently encouraging her to look up.

"Please, M'lady," the woman said quietly, handing her a kerchief. "Please, find no disfavor with us. We didn't mean to hurt you. We didn't mean to--"

"No!" Vala cried, "No, please, don't think I am upset with you. I'm not. It's just...well, you, this place, it reminds me of those things that I do not have. It's not your fault. I begrudge you nothing." She wiped her tears on the kerchief, and rose.

Elaewen didn't look convinced as she shared a glance with her husband, who now held the baby. Vala extended her arms to the baby.

"May I hold her?"

Frayhan hesitated only briefly, then, with a smile of pleasure, placed the child in Vala's arms. The infant grinned up at her and made a soft cooing sound.

"Oh, she's beautiful," Vala murmured. "What's her name?"

Elaewen and Frayhan again exchanged looks, before Frayhan spoke. "We would be honored, M'lady, if you chose a name for her. She has not yet been christened. She has no God-given name."

Vala looked up at him, astonished by his request. "You would let me name your child?"

"We would be highly honored if you would," Elaewen replied.

Vala studied them both for a long moment. If this was indeed the land that Severrani was from she could understand why he yearned for it. What she couldn't understand was why he had left it in the first place, and why he had said there was nothing here for him. It seemed to have everything she had ever dreamt of. Even though she did not consider herself a faery, these people did. And to allow her into their home, to speak to her with such kindness and reverence, to even ask that she name their child--it was almost too much to comprehend.

She turned her gaze on the infant, again taken with the resemblance to Lawanda's child. Perhaps this was her spirit reborn. Maybe she had never made it to the faery realm, but had instead been reborn into this gentle soul. Vala clung to that hope and dream.

"Laraliwyn," she murmured, though where the name had sprang from she wasn't sure.

"Laraliwyn," Elaewen repeated with a smile. "What a beautiful name. What does it mean, M'lady?"

Vala paused, then wondered at her own words as they tumbled from her lips without thought. "It means 'gift of the heavens, blessed by the fae'."

Both Elaewen and Frayhan caught their breath. Tears flooded Elaewen's eyes and cascaded down her cheeks. She fell to her knees before Vala.

"Thank you, M'lady," she whispered. "Thank you."

Vala blushed. "Please, don't bow before me. I am only Vala, a visitor to your home."

"But our home is surely blessed by your presence," Frayhan put in, his voice cracking with emotion.

"As I am blessed by your friendship and acceptance," Vala said, then suddenly sagged against the table as her head reeled.

Elaewen rose swiftly and took the baby from her. "M'lady! You are not well?"

"I--I'm just tired," Vala managed as Frayhan helped her sit. "I haven't eaten for a while, and I am still very thirsty."

"Then let's get food on the table at once," Elaewen said, and promptly began to issue orders to her husband and the children. Within moments, a simple yet delicious meal was spread before Vala. She ate slowly, trying to remember her manners, yet so hungry she could have devoured most of the food on the table. The children talked and laughed and teased each other as they ate. Elaewen and Frayhan were quieter, though they answered any question Vala asked them.

She learned that the people now inhabiting Gannabrina were third generation of the original settlers, and that, though they were of the same bloodlines, their beliefs were far different.

While the first settlers had scarred the land with their greed, the people now living here respected the land and all that was on it. They bemoaned the fact that the fae had left their country, and they wished with all of their hearts that the faery realm would once again look with favor on the large island they called home.

Vala began to wonder just how long it had been since Severrani had been here, whether he knew of these people and their gentle, accepting ways, their love for the fae. She wished she could tell him, wished she could erase that pain she had seen in his eyes when he stared across the sea.

Thoughts of Severrani brought thoughts of Lawanda and of Vala's promise to Tyrs. As much as she wished she could just stay in Gannabrina, become a member of the society here, she knew she had to return to Larendalath and find Lawanda.

But how?

Chapter Eight

The wind blew gently across the fields, ruffling Vala's hair. Without looking at it or touching it, she knew it was no longer tangling. Just as Severrani's hair had refused to tangle on the wind. Her gaze traveled forlornly over the sea before her. He was on the other side, in another world, yet she could not keep her thoughts away from him. Even her dreams the previous night had included him. She could not explain to herself why he had suddenly become so important to her. *He shouldn't be,* she thought. *After all, I was only his prisoner, someone he planned to turn over to the king.* But did he have a choice? The law of his king bound him, just as the law of hers had bound her.

She huffed out an irritated breath. Why couldn't she keep her thoughts away from him? Perhaps it had something to do with being here, in Gannabrina. Or perhaps...she reached up to touch at her hair. She knew without a mirror that it was white, as white as Severrani's and Aric's. But how? She was not fae, she was human. So much didn't make sense. How could she have come here? How could she have known what to name the baby? And know what it meant? How could she now look as she did? She sighed and sat down in the grass.

Elaewen and Frayhan had insisted that she stay the night, and had offered her their bed. She had refused, but had agreed to sleep in one of the children's beds. She had not wanted to inconvenience them, either, but Vaedon was so honored at having a fae sleeping in his bed she couldn't turn him down.

It was strange the way faeries were accepted, even worshipped, here in Gannabrina, while in her own land they were now considered demons. She again wondered why Severrani had left Gannabrina, what had caused him to abandon such a place. She had asked Elaewen and Frayhan if they knew of Severrani or any of the words on the medallion. All she had found out was that Gannabribriel was a fae. They knew nothing else about him, but had said that an elder in the village might have more information, and they had gone to town to fetch the old woman. While waiting, Vala had gone to the cliffs, drawn there by an unexplainable urge to see the water, hear the crash of the waves, smell the salt air. Before her fall from the cliffs outside of Strander, she had never seen the ocean, yet now it gave her a sense of peace. Just as this land did. She felt at home, as if she had always been here.

With a heavy sigh, she let her thoughts drift to Gannabribriel. She had a strange feeling about him, as if she should know of him. And perhaps she did - in her heart and soul. Had the Outsider been Gannabribriel? Although recent rumors in the village had called him both fae and demon, Vala's mother had never mentioned the Outsider might have been fae. Wouldn't she have? Vala sighed. Perhaps not. It was bad enough to be saved *from* the fairies, but to be saved *by* a faery? Vala suspected her hard life would have been even worse.

But what had happened to the Outsider? Vala did not know. She had heard so many different accounts of his disappearance, she could not even guess. All she knew was that the relief had been widespread when he had gone. Vala was sure her mother had not felt the same way, however. She could vividly remember the sadness that had descended upon her mother at any mention of the Outsider. And she could also remember the friction that sadness had caused between her parents. Her father did not share whatever the Outsider had meant to her mother. Vala shuddered, considering the possibilities that her mother had been drawn to the Outsider as a married woman should not have been. But what did it matter now? They were all gone. All of them. Hopefully, they had settled their differences in the afterlife.

Prea had followed her from the cottage and now snuffled at her neck. Vala laughed and reached up to scratch the pony between its tufted ears, then got to her feet, and shook the dirt and grain from the skirts Elaewen had given her. She brushed her cheek against the soft shawl she wore, one made by Elaewen. It reminded her of her mother, but instead of bringing grief it brought her peace, as if her mother had guided Elaewen's hand in making it.

They were such a kind family, so accommodating, so open and accepting. Vala wished she had something to give them in payment, but they continually told her that her presence was enough. Though it embarrassed her, it also pleased her. She glanced toward the cottage, surprised to find that she instinctively knew the family was returning. She turned her steps in that direction, and arrived at the cottage just moments before the wagon appeared on the rutted lane leading from town. Frayhan reined in and leapt from the bench to assist an elderly woman down. The woman peered at Vala through watery blue eyes. Strands of white hair had escaped the colorful cloth wrap she wore, and a toothless smile crinkled her aged face. She reached out to grasp Vala's hand in greeting.

Vala smiled, overwhelmed by a profound sense of peace and acceptance, as if she were a long-lost relative being welcomed home.

"This is Vala," Frayhan introduced. "Vala, this is Ybrilla. Perhaps she can help you with your questions."

"Thank you for coming," Vala said, gently squeezing the old woman's hand.

"It is my honor to serve you," Ybrilla returned.

"Come," Elaewen said, joining them. "Inside, where I can make some tea, and you can sit down." She led the others into the cottage.

Elaewen put the baby in her cradle, then shooed the children outside to chores, before busying herself with tea preparation. Frayhan helped Ybrilla to a seat at the table, then went to the hearth to help Elaewen. Vala sat down across from the old woman. She folded her hands on the table in front of her, and began, eager to find out what Ybrilla knew.

"I am new here," she started, "and I am seeking some information on Gannabribriel. I believe he may have lived here at one time, as did a fae by the name of Severrani."

"And what makes you believe this?" Ybrilla asked.

Vala shrugged. "I'm not sure. It's just a...feeling. Severrani now resides in Larendalath, but I believe his heart is still yearning for Gannabrina."

Ybrilla studied her a moment, then nodded. "I think you are right. Gannabribriel was the Elthea, a powerful healer, both of spirit and of body. It is said that his only son followed in his way, with a gift of healing that was just as strong."

Vala stared at her, mouth agape. "Son?"

Ybrilla nodded. "Severrani was said to be the only son of Gannabribriel."

Vala quickly re-gathered her senses. "What happened to Gannabribriel?"

Ybrilla shrugged her bony shoulders. "No one knows for sure. He died in Lareriveth."

"In Lareriveth? Where?"

"In a mountain village called Strander."

Vala felt the color drain from her face. "When?" she breathed.

"It's been about nineteen years now," Ybrilla said quietly, her gaze fixed on Vala.

Vala stared at her, stunned. The pieces fell into place so swiftly it left her reeling. Gannabribriel *was* the Outsider. She was certain of it. Was it possible that he had died at the hands of her people? If so, no wonder Severrani held her in such contempt. The thought tore at her heart. She had to get back to Severrani, had to find out if this was indeed true and, if so, had to apologize for her people's actions. She regarded Ybrilla thoughtfully. "You seem to know much of the fae world."

"Aye," the old woman agreed.

"What happened here? Why did they leave?"

Ybrilla glanced toward Elaewen and Frayhan, who were busy at the hearth. Then Ybrilla leaned forward, placed one thin, soft hand atop Vala's, and looked her in the eyes. "Do you think they have?" she whispered, and pushed up one side of her cloth cap to reveal slightly pointed ears.

Vala gasped. Ybrilla was fae. And if she was here, there must be others. But where were they? She started to ask, but Ybrilla shushed her with a gnarled finger to her lips, as Elaewen brought the tea to the table.

"I must return to Larendalath," Vala said finally. "But I don't know how. Can you help me?"

"Why do you want to return?" Ybrilla asked, sitting back.

"I...I have made promises that I need to keep."

Ybrilla tipped her head, studying Vala. "Promises to keep, or promises to fulfill?"

"I don't understand."

The old woman smiled and again patted her hand. "You will. And, as you have said, you must return." She looked to Frayhan in question. "What say you, Frayhan? How may your guest return to the land across the sea?"

He rubbed at his chin. "There is the boat," he said finally. "It could sail as early as tomorrow."

"A boat?" Vala echoed, remembering Severrani's look of longing when she had mentioned boats. "I've never been on a boat before. Will it take long?"

"No," Frayhan told her. "At least, it won't take long to get to the shores of Lareriveth. But from there to the Faery Realm of Larendalath, I cannot say. That will be up to you and you alone."

Vala's hand strayed to the medallion about her neck. "No, not alone," she murmured. "I will have Gannabribriel's spirit to keep me company."

Morning came bright and sunny, with a brisk easterly wind. Frayhan commented on that as being in the fae's favor with the voyage Vala was about to undertake. For her part, Vala was nervous, not quite sure how to view the huge wooden structure that bobbed on the waves at the dock.

Tall poles of varying thickness rose from the deck of the ship, each connected to another in a confusing tangle of rope and sail. A row of small holes ran along the side of the ship, though she had no idea what they were for. She only hoped they stayed well above the level of the water. The thought of being leagues from land with only the wooden ship between her and the power of the sea sent a chill racing through her. She wondered how deep the ocean was. She had never thought to ask Severrani. Still, it had to be fairly deep to allow such a vessel as the one before her to float on it. And exactly how did it float? With all of the crates and barrels being loaded onto the ship, she was sure it would sink straight out of sight. She wasn't sure she wanted to entrust her life to it. Still, what choice did she have? If she was going to get back to Larendalath, she had to first get back to the mainland. She clutched the medallion and watched the men rushing on and off the ship via a long stretch of wood. Frayhan's voice startled her.

"It's almost time to board, M'lady," he said.

"This is so exciting!" Aerawin cried, clapping her small hands. "I should like to go on a ship someday, Papa. Will you take me?"

Frayhan smiled at her, then scooped her up in his strong arms. "Someday, perhaps, my sweet. Until then, we'll have to pray that Vala will return and tell us all the story of her journey to Lareriveth and Larendalath."

Vala tugged at the heavy hood that hid her hair from view. Elaewen had suggested she wear the hooded cloak, else her departure might be severely delayed by the well-wishes of the villagers. Already, several of them had cast her awestruck glances before whispering excitedly behind their hands to their companions. The mood on the docks seemed very jovial and boisterous.

"Is it always this busy?" Vala asked.

"No." Frayhan grinned at her. "But I suspect that a rumor might have gotten round about a faery being on this ship."

Vala frowned, not sure how to take that. Although Frayhan and Elaewen had assured her that faeries were adored and welcomed by all in Gannabrina, Vala still held misgivings. It was hard to forget the chains that had bound her, harder still to forget the sentence of death that had been leveled at her. She shrank back into the shadows of the building they stood against as a tall, muscular man approached.

"Frayhan," he greeted, his gaze on Vala. "Is this the passenger?"

"Aye, she is," Frayhan replied. "You'll treat her with utmost care, I'm sure."

The man peered at Vala, then smiled warmly. "Aye, a faery is always welcome aboard a ship, Frayhan. You know that." He bowed to Vala. "My name is Tholian. I am the captain on this voyage. Might I escort you aboard?"

Vala suddenly froze, her heart racing wildly. What if they found out she wasn't a faery? Or worse, what if they found out she was? By the Saints, she didn't know if being a fae was a good thing or not, anymore. She turned to Frayhan and gripped his arm, though words seemed to stick in her throat. He patted her shoulder in reassurance, obviously not understanding the cause for her alarm.

"Tholian is the best captain in these waters, M'lady," he said softly.

"That's not it," Vala murmured, fighting back the tears that threatened. "It's this place, these people, this land...all of you." She swallowed hard, trying to talk past the lump in her throat. "I shall miss you all dearly."

He smiled at her. "Then you shall have to return."

Vala forced a smile to her lips, then stood on tiptoe to kiss the cheek of the little girl he held in his arms. "Where is Vaedon?" Vala asked Aerawin.

"I don't know. He was exploring," Aerawin answered, placing her small hand over Vala's kiss.

"Frayhan!" Elaewen hurried toward them, her face worried. "I can't find Vaedon. I've searched everywhere for him."

Frayhan put Aerawin down. "I'll look. He's probably amongst the cargo packers. He likes to badger them about their wares." He looked at Vala. "Godspeed, M'lady. May your journey be swift and rewarding and may you return here, to your home, soon."

Vala's pulse quickened at the words. Home? Here? Yes, it did feel right. She smiled at him, then, on impulse, kissed his cheek as well. He seemed as surprised and delighted as Aerawin had been and hurried away to search for his son, his cheeks flaming.

Elaewen regarded Vala for a moment, then abruptly gathered her close. Vala clung to her, feeling safe, warm and loved for the first time since losing her parents. She hated leaving, hating facing the unknown yet again, but drew strength from the knowledge that she now had a home to come back to.

"I wish I could say goodbye to Vaedon," she said quietly. "I will miss all of you. I feel as if I have known you forever instead of just two days."

"We will miss you as well," Elaewen said, standing back. "And we will look forward to your swift return."

Vala turned to Aerawin and gave her another kiss. "That's for your brother. Give it to him when you find him, will you?"

"I will!" Aerawin declared, placing her other hand over the kiss. "I shall hold on to them both until I see you again."

Vala couldn't help but smile. She turned to Tholian. "I guess I'm ready, then."

He nodded, took her by the arm and guided her through the throngs of people to the gangplank. She hesitated briefly, glancing at the dark waters that lapped the dock and the sides of the ship, but Tholian's grip was steady, and he led her up the plank to the deck. As soon as she was safely aboard, the crewmembers pulled the gangplank up. There was no going back now.

Vala turned to wave goodbye to those on shore. The wind chose that moment to gust and tore her hood from her head. Her white hair swirled out behind her, drawing cries and gasps from the crowd on the docks. All turned her way. The crewmembers stood in momentary shock, until Tholian issued them orders in a firm voice. At once they returned to the business of setting sail.

Vala gripped the railing as the boat slowly left Gannabrina behind. She was surprised at how much the vessel swayed and bobbed as it headed out of the cove toward open sea. Already her stomach was beginning to rebel at the unfamiliar motion. She looked over as one of the crewmen came forward, nervously clutching his cap before him.

"M'lady," he murmured, tipping his head. "The captain says I should show you your cabin."

"Thank you. I would appreciate that." Vala let loose of the railing, then cried out as she was nearly thrown to the deck.

The crewman grabbed her, keeping her from falling. "Easy now," he warned. "It can take some time to get your sea legs."

"So, I see," Vala returned, gripping his arm. She gave him a weak smile. "And we aren't even at sea yet."

He smiled back and escorted her across the deck and down a narrow flight of stairs. Her room was small, holding two bunks fastened to the wall, and a small table bolted to the floor.

"We're not a passenger ship, M'lady," the crewman apologized. "If there is anything you need to make your stay more comfortable, please let us know."

"Thank you," Vala replied. She didn't tell him how this was bigger than the room she'd had at Lawanda's home, and infinitely better than sleeping outside in the cold and rain.

He bobbed his head at her again and retreated, pulling the door closed behind him.

Vala clung to the berth, one hand pressed against her stomach, the other tight about the wood frame beside her, and wondered if there was someplace to retch. She carefully lowered herself to the lower berth, and lay back. The bunk had been piled thick with blankets, and she nestled gratefully into their warmth and security. It took several moments of fierce determination to calm the nausea, and when it finally abated, she was again flooded with heartache. She already missed Gannabrina and wished with all of her heart that she had not had to leave it. But she had made a promise to Tyrs, a promise she would keep.

She closed her eyes, her thoughts on Ybrilla. 'Promises to keep, promises to fullfill', the woman had said. What had she meant by that? Vala opened her eyes, drew out the medallion and turned it over. Well, now she knew that Kjavli was a place, that Elthea meant healer, and that Gannabribriel was a person. And not just a person--Severrani's father. A man killed by Vala's own neighbors. She grimaced, then abruptly wondered how her mother had fit into the equation. Why had Gannabribriel given her the medallion? Or had he?

The unpleasant thought flitted through Vala's mind. It was immediately dislodged. What if her mother had taken it? Stolen it from the dying fae? No! Her mother would never do such a thing! She believed in the fae, believed in their goodness. But did she really? Were the small gifts to the fae delivered out of faith or fear? Perhaps her generosity was nothing more than a bribe. And what was that Tyrs had said?

Vala sat up, the memory coming back to her in a rush. *I thought pleasing you would make things different for us. I thought perhaps you would show gratitude.* By the Gods! How could she have not understood? Tyrs and Lawanda had let her into their home, had provided for her, just to placate her! *Keep the fae happy, and no bad things will happen to you! Including the death of your own child!* Tyrs had placed the blame directly on her. The thought seared through Vala's heart, and tears leapt to her eyes.

But what of Lawanda? Was she thinking the same way as her husband? Or had she truly befriended Vala with no thoughts of payment? Vala didn't know. But one thing she did know--she had to find Lawanda and return her to her home. Even if Tyrs didn't deserve it.

The boat was two days out and still Vala had not grown accustomed to the motion. The ship's cook had given her an ample supply of dried raspberries to quell her nausea, but Vala was having a hard time even eating those. Tholian assured her that the feeling of unease would eventually pass. Vala was beginning to doubt it.

She had not been on deck since the boat had set sail, too unsure of her stomach to attempt it. She lay on the berth, eyes closed against the swaying of the lamp hanging from the ceiling.

A tap on the door brought her eyes open. "Come in," she called weakly.

The door opened and Tholian stepped inside, carrying a child whom Vala recognized instantly. Vaedon! She sat up carefully, willing her stomach to remain calm.

"M'lady," Tholian said, "I hate to intrude, but one of my crewmen just found Vaedon hidden amongst the crates and barrels in the hold. I'm afraid he is quite ill. He has been without food and water these two days, and I believe that whatever he had in his stomach before leaving Gannabrina he has long since lost. He has a fever as well. I was wondering if you...well, if you had any magic you could work on him to help him recover."

Vala stared at the child in despair. His small face was pale, beaded with sweat, his eyes barely open, his lips cracked and red. His clothing reeked of oil, sweat and vomitus. He turned his head in her direction, and though he said nothing she could almost feel his pleading for help. Forgetting her own unease, she rose.

"Lay him here, on the bed," she instructed. "Fetch me some cool water for him, and something clean for him to wear."

Tholian nodded and hurried away. Vala sat down beside Vaedon and took his small hand in hers. She offered him a smile.

"Now see what your inquisitiveness got you into?" she asked softly.

"I only wanted to be with you," he whispered. "And...I wanted to see Larendalath, too."

Tears stood in his eyes, tears that Vala was actually glad to see. It meant that he was not severely dehydrated. She brushed the hair from his sweaty forehead, wondering what she could do to ease his sufferings. The lamplight caught the red stone in the medallion, and Vala looked at it thoughtfully. Perhaps it held the answer. After all, it had belonged to the most gifted healer in all of Gannabrina. Maybe there was still some power left in it, something she could use to help Vaedon. But how would she access that power?

She wrapped her hand around the medallion, then closed her eyes, letting her mind drift where it willed. At first there was nothing more than her own scattered and confused thoughts but slowly they settled. She could almost picture a light mist, white in color, as it swirled and flowed, finally creating words. She frowned, puzzled, but laid her other hand on Vaedon's belly, and spoke the words.

"Power of earth, power of fae, come together in this way. Blessed be the power to cure, strength and wellness will endure."

A gentle warmth played about the hand clutching the medallion. Red light flowed through her clenched fingers, came to rest on her other hand. The warmth seemed to move from one hand to the other. Vaedon wriggled beneath her, his brow furrowed with confusion. Then, abruptly, he exhaled, his relief evident. A smile flashed across his face.

"Saints!" he breathed, then clapped one hand over his mouth as if to quell the use of a swear word. His eyes went large.

Vala laughed. "I'll say nothing of your transgression to your father," she told him. "I think you'll have enough explaining to do as to why you are here and not at home."

Vaedon grimaced, sitting up. He gripped Vala's hand. "Can you somehow use your magic and tell my mama and papa that I'm all right? I didn't mean to worry them. I only wanted to see the ship, and maybe..."

"You were wrong, Vaedon," Vala told him. "You know that. Your parents are probably worried sick over your disappearance. Somehow I have to let them know you're safe." She got up as the door to her cabin once again opened.

Tholian stepped inside carrying a waterskin and an armful of clean clothes. He looked at Vaedon in surprise and relief, then bowed his head at Vala.

"Thank you, M'lady," he said. "Here are the clothes you asked for, and the water. But he looks so much better."

"He'll be fine now. Still, he needs rest and fluids to recover fully." She looked at Vaedon. "Change into the clean clothes, freshen up with the water, then I want you to take a nap."

"A nap?" he whined. "But I'm too old for naps!"

Vala kept her smile to herself. "No, you're not. You'll nap. Captain Tholian, I would like to go up on deck."

He nodded, stepping aside to let her pass. She gave Vaedon one last parental glance, then walked past Tholian toward the stairs. She was surprised and vastly relieved to find that when she had settled Vaedon's stomach her own queasiness had ceased. The rocking motion of the ship no longer bothered her, and she climbed the steps, eager to be free of the confines of the cabin, to feel the wind upon her face. She didn't even want to think about how she had used the fae magic.

The wind on deck blew briskly, filling the large white sails to capacity. Vala stared up at them, watching the men scamper across the rigging with the same sureness of foot mountain goats had on their slopes. Gulls soared after the ship, diving and swooping into the wake.

"What are the birds doing?" she asked Tholian.

"Feeding. The ship churns the water up. Food floats closer to the top and the gulls can get it easier."

"How clever," Vala murmured, approaching the railing. She watched the birds for a moment, one hand closed about the medallion. Finally, she turned to Tholian. "Have you some parchment and a quill?"

He frowned in question but nodded. "I shall fetch them for you at once."

He hurried away and Vala returned her attention to the birds. How graceful they were, floating on the air currents. Their timing seemed faultless. Never did they fly too close to the ship or become entangled in the ropes or sails. In fact, several of them had landed on the railing and were studying Vala with the same degree of curiosity as she regarded them.

"M'lady?" Tholian returned with parchment, a quill and a pot of ink, holding them out to her.

Vala took them and quickly penned a letter to Elaewen and Frayhan. When the ink had dried, she rolled up the small piece of parchment. Not completely understanding her own actions she pulled out several strands of her hair. One of these she tied around the parchment roll, as easily as if it were yarn, then she looked at one of the gulls sitting on the railing. The bird sidestepped to stop directly in front of her. With the second strand of hair, she tied the parchment carefully to the bird's leg.

"All right," she said softly. "I want you to deliver this to Frayhan Helassi in Gannabrina. It is very important that he receive it. My blessing goes with you."

The bird bowed its head, then sprang from the railing and soared away over the sea. Tholian stared after it, his awe apparent. Vala glanced at him uneasily, only now realizing how strange her actions must seem. And not only to him. They were equally as surprising and frightening to her. And, yet, how natural they had seemed.

"I need to check on Vaedon," she said and hurried back toward her room.

The little boy was sound asleep, obviously more exhausted from his ordeal than he had been willing to admit. Vala covered him with a blanket, then sat down beside him. So many strange things were happening. Things she did not understand, perhaps did not want to. She sighed, her heart heavy with despair. Who was she? Was she even human? She was beginning to doubt that. Foreign words and strange actions, even the use of magic, seemed to be coming easily to her. Why? She looked down at the medallion. Why now, after all of these years, was it answering to her call? Heeding her desires? Perhaps everything was due to being in the Faery Realm in Larendalath. She didn't know anyone else who had gone there and returned. Perhaps they too would have been changed. She curled up beside Vaedon, placing one arm protectively about his small body. His warmth and the gentle swaying of the ship soon lulled her to sleep.

Her dreams were scattered and confusing. She thought she saw Severrani, but at the same time she knew it was not he. Images of her cottage, of her mother and father, of Lawanda and Aric, flitted in and out of her awareness. The medallion glowed like a red beacon, but she had no idea where it drew her. Hard, evil faces of the citizens of Strander swarmed around her, cutting her off from those she sought, those she truly loved. Words, at once mysterious and familiar, embedded themselves into her exhausted mind, like imprints left in wet sand.

She woke with a start, heart racing, muscles tight and cramped. Vaedon murmured in his sleep and snuggled closer to her warmth. The room had grown quite chilly with the coming of night, and Vala quickly snagged another blanket from the end of the berth. She wrapped it around herself and Vaedon, then pulled him close against her.

She wondered what she would do with him once they reached land. She was reluctant to leave him with Tholian. The captain might not want a child wandering about the ship, getting in the way. And would he be able to keep a close eye on Vaedon? Make sure he didn't sneak off to follow her? She looked down at the golden hair that glowed in the lamplight and wondered if the boy would listen to her, obey her. She would have to try to convince him to wait here, to be obedient.

A soft tap on her door roused her, and she carefully crawled away from Vaedon to answer. Tholian stood in the hallway, wool cap in his hands.

"M'lady," he said quietly, as if he knew Vaedon slept, "you wanted to be alerted when we got close to land."

"We're there already?" Vala murmured. She had thought she would have more time to think, to formulate a plan. Now, it seemed, she would have to plan while she walked. She glanced over her shoulder at Vaedon, then stepped into the hallway with Tholian, keeping her voice low and pulling the door shut behind her.

"About the boy," she began.

Tholian smiled. "You've no need to worry over him, M'lady. I've known Frayhan for many years. I've known his son since birth. He'll be welcome to stay on board. I've already talked to two of my crew about taking on the task of watching over him. He'll not be leaving this ship unless I know about it."

Vala smiled, greatly relieved. "Thank you, Tholian. That eases my mind."

He paused, fingering his hat. "And what of you, M'lady? Where will you go now? What supplies might you be needing?"

Vala frowned. "Not a lot, really. A small pack with water and some food. Enough to last for several days. Oh, and some proper clothing for walking. Might you have some breeches and a tunic that I could use? And some boots?"

"Aye, I think I can find something that would fit you. As for the pack, consider it done." He paused again, obviously unsure of continuing.

Vala touched his arm lightly. "And?" she prompted.

He started at her touch, but did not pull away. "Your hair, M'lady. I have heard some ghastly stories about how Lareriveth views the fae. It might be wise to try to cover as much of your hair as possible, though I know that you have your magic to assist you."

My magic, Vala thought. What magic? She nodded, again pushing the uneasy thoughts aside. "Yes, you're right. I have the cloak from Elaewen. That should suffice."

"And when will you be wanting a ship back to Gannabrina?"

This time it was Vala who paused. "I--I don't know," she replied. "I don't want to interfere with your schedule. Carry on as you would normally. If I can make it back for your next sailing, then I shall endeavor to do so. If not, I shall be forced to find another passage."

He nodded, bowed and took his leave. Vala turned to open the door, and as she did so, she heard Vaedon scuffle back to bed. With a small smile, she entered. The boy was stretched out, the blanket pulled halfway over his head. Vala approached quietly, then poked his side, eliciting a startled giggle. He threw the blanket back and looked up at her.

"You're going to leave me here, aren't you?" he asked.

"I have no other choice, Vaedon," she told him. "You can't come with me. It's too dangerous."

"But, Vala," he whined, sitting up and clutching her hand in his, "I wanted to see Larendalath, the land of the faeries. Please, take me with you, please."

"I can't, Vaedon. If I could, rest assured I would. Now, you must be obedient and stay here with Captain Tholian."

Vaedon pouted, crossing his arms tightly over his small chest. "That's not fair! If I'm to be punished by Papa when I get home, at the least I should have something to show for it."

"But you do," Vala replied, laughing. "You've been aboard a great ship, out to sea. If you're very good, I'll talk to the captain about letting you go ashore and explore the beach. But I must have your promise that you will not try to follow me. All right?"

He said nothing, and she tilted his face up to look into his brown eyes.

"All right?" she asked again.

Vaedon huffed out an irritated breath and nodded. Vala gave him a stern look, and the little boy murmured a soft, "Yes."

Vala ruffled his hair and gave him a hug. "Thank you, Vaedon," she said quietly. "I couldn't bear to see anything happen to you."

He drew back and looked up into her face. "And I can't stand the thought of anything happening to you, either. Promise that you'll come back to see me? Promise?"

Vala hesitated, then nodded. "I promise, Vaedon," she said, though just how she would keep that promise she didn't know.

Vala gripped her pack tightly and waited for the gangplank to be set to the dock. A stiff breeze blew against her back, threatening to push her off the ship before she was ready. Vaedon stood nearby, his hands in the firm grip of two of Captain Tholian's men. He wore a grim expression, but no grimmer than the two crewmen, who were obviously not thrilled to be assigned as guards to a child.

The dock was a busy place, swarming with people from all over Lareriveth. It was the first time Vala had ever been to the seaside port, and she was overwhelmed with the sheer energy of the place. Her gaze traveled to the mountains. Her village of Strander was somewhere up there, though she had no idea where. In some ways, she hoped it was very far away, yet she still felt she owed Tyrs an apology and an explanation for her failure to yet fulfill her promise to him. She hoped that he had not suffered a punishment for letting her go, but reality assured her he had. Guilt bore heavily on her as she turned her gaze on Vaedon.

His small face was puckered, his dark eyes shiny with tears. She lowered her pack to the deck and went towards him, hunkering down in front of him. The crewmen released their grips, and Vaedon flung himself into her arms. She held tightly to him, stroking his hair.

"Now, you promised," she whispered. "You promised me that you would obey my wishes."

"I--I know," he sobbed. "But it just hurts to let you go."

"I know, Vaedon. It hurts me, too, but at least I know you are safe." She held him away from her and gently wiped his cheeks dry with the long sleeve of her tunic.

Though Tholian had attempted to find her something that would fit, he had been unable to. The pants were too big, the sleeves of the tunic too long. Still, it would be far easier to wear than the skirts she had been given by Elaewen. An idea suddenly occurred to her, and she looked Vaedon in the eye.

"You know, your mama loaned me some very fine clothing while I was at your cottage. I've left it in my cabin. Could I entrust you to make sure that your mama gets it back? It would mean a lot to me. Would you do this for me?"

Vaedon's face brightened and he nodded. "I will," he said.

"Good. I knew I could count on you to do this." She wished she had something to give him, to remind him of her, but all she had that was truly hers was the medallion, and even that had belonged to someone else. She kissed him gently on both cheeks, then straightened.

The crewmen immediately regained his hands, as if they thought he would dash down the gangplank and be gone before they could move. Vala gave them both a smile of gratitude and reclaimed her pack as Captain Tholian came toward her.

"Are you ready, M'lady?" he asked, offering her his arm.

"Yes." She gave Vaedon one last look, then allowed Tholian to help her down the ramp to solid ground.

She was immediately grateful for the hood on the cloak. Throngs of people crushed against her as they went about their business on the busy docks. She knew were they to glimpse her hair there would have been a different response to her presence, and she didn't for one moment think it would be as kind as the reception she had received in Gannabrina. Tholian guided her with a sure hand to the edge of the village, where the numbers of people were fewer.

"This is where I must leave you, M'lady," he said softly. "I wish I did not have to, but..."

"I understand," Vala replied, though her heart quickened at the thought of being alone again. Her gaze traveled to the ship. She could see Vaedon hanging onto the railing, staring toward her, the crewmen at his side. Something about the boy's posture told her that the task of watching after his mama's clothing would not be enough to keep him on board. But what else could she give him? Unless... she looked back at Tholian. "Do you have a bit of string or leather?"

He shrugged, fumbling about in his pockets. Finally, he pulled a seaman's pendant from under his shirt. "I have this," he offered, tugging on the black leather lace that held the pendant.

Vala hesitated, not wanting him to part with something that no doubt meant a lot to him. "No, that's all right." She slipped the medallion from her neck and studied the chain. She had never, in all of the years she had owned it, seen a way to unclasp it. Now was no different. She sighed. She had hoped that maybe such an expensive bit of jewelry would entice Vaedon to do her bidding. If only she had something, anything... She gasped as the chain suddenly separated, pulling apart as if it had heard her thoughts, possessed a life of its own. She swallowed hard, removed the medallion, then watched in fascination as the chain resealed itself. Tholian sucked in his breath in astonishment, then started when she abruptly held the chain out to him.

"Give this to Vaedon," she instructed. "Tell him that I don't want to lose it and I felt it would be safer with him than with me."

Tholian took the chain from her, his hands trembling, his eyes wide with awe. "I shall do so," he said. "And don't worry about him following you, M'Lady. He won't."

Vala smiled, tucking the medallion into her breast pocket. "I only wanted to make the parting easier for Vaedon."

"I'm afraid that even this chain will not do that," the captain told her softly, then hesitated. "And what of your medallion?" He quickly removed his seaman's pendant and held out the leather tie to her. "Please, take it, M'Lady. I would be humbled."

Vala sighed, truly touched at his sacrifice as she accepted the leather cord. "Thank you, Captain, for everything. I truly do appreciate it. And I shall find some way to repay you for your kindness."

"Your presence on my ship is payment enough, for surely it has been blessed."

Vala blushed, smiled, then turned and strode away. She refused to look back, refused to see either Tholian's face or Vaedon's. Tears obscured her vision for many steps, and she hurried her pace, clutching the neck of the cloak. Although she was eager to be out of the city, where she would go she didn't know.

The woods outside the city were cool and dark, and Vala drew her cloak tighter, huddling into its warmth and security. She felt as if unseen eyes watched her every movement, every step. She had no weapon and chastised herself for not asking Tholian for one. She searched the pack hopefully, but realized that Tholian expected her to rely on her magic more than on a man-made weapon. It was a foolish oversight on her part, and she was sure she would pay the penalty for it.

She kept her pace quick and true, not exactly sure where she traveled, yet guided by some inner voice. It was not until late evening that she finally stopped to rest. Even then, she didn't really want to. The woods were too confining, too dark and close. They pressed against her, surrounded her, watched her. They were very unlike the forest Severrani had taken her into, and she suddenly realized why. Though they lived, growing and thriving, they were not alive. Without the magic of the Faery Realm surrounding them, caressing them, they were only wood and greenery, with no spirit. They did not comfort, only frighten. She huddled against a bumpy trunk, her gaze darting from tree to brush to rock. Pursuers could be hidden almost anywhere.

Pursuers? She forced a grim smile to her lips. What pursuers? No one knew she was here. She took a long pull from her waterskin, grimacing at the sour taste of the water. Strange. She had drank from Severrani's bag only a few times, yet she now preferred the taste of fae water over what she carried. Just another sure sign she was now no longer a human. The thought sent a burn of regret through her, and at the same time a thrill of delight. She shook her head at her own confusion, took out the medallion and strung it on the leather tie, tying the knot as tightly as she could.

She studied the stone in the fading daylight, watching it catch and reflect the last traces of sun. She turned it over and traced the engraved words with her thumb. So, 'Elthea' meant 'High Healer'. High Healer Gannabribriel. She wondered what Ithys meant. Ithys Kjvali. High Healer Gannabribriel of Kjvali? Ithys could be any number of words. Still, speaking it with Gannabrina had sent her to the wonderful land. So, 'Ithys' might mean 'take me to'? She shook her head and dug into her pack for the salt pork and dried fruit Tholian had provided. The meat was almost as repulsive as the water, but she managed to swallow several bites. She longed to taste the sweet brown bread that Aric and Severrani had given her.

The thought of Severrani brought again a pang of loneliness, and Vala hurriedly repacked her supplies. She didn't want to think of him, not now. She couldn't understand why she harbored such feelings for a man she didn't even know, one who was willing to turn her over to the fae king in a heartbeat. He didn't want her, didn't have any such attachment to her. That much was clear. Why should she torture herself with unrequited love?

Love? She amazed herself with that thought.

She got to her feet, determined to find the gate that would allow her entrance to the fae world. But where? And how? She frowned, trying to remember what it was that allowed her to reach the Faery Realm before. And how she had gotten to Gannabrina. Was it simply that she had said those words? Did she have to be in the Funeral Meadow then? Both times she had gone to the Faery Realm, she had traveled from the meadow. She supposed Aric had opened the doorway the first time, but what about the second time? She remembered screaming for help, calling for Aric or Severrani. Had one of them heard her pleas and opened the door? She didn't know, and she was too unsure to test the medallion just yet.

She walked until it grew too dark to clearly see her footing, then chose a place to rest. Several large trees grew in a cluster and Vala crawled into the small space between them, then sat hunched with her cloak drawn tightly about her. Sounds came out of the darkness, and she tried to identify them, convincing herself there was bravery in knowledge.

However, most of the sounds she did not recognize. She hadn't paid much attention to the sounds of the forest when she was with Severrani and Aric. It hadn't seemed so threatening then. Growing up in a meadow, with only a thin copse of alder trees, didn't afford her the knowledge of what creatures lurked about.

A strange hooting sound startled her, and her gaze jerked upwards. All right, she had heard that sound before. An owl. There had been some small barn owls that had taken up residence in one of the storage buildings in Strander. This one sounded quite a bit larger and heavier, but, still, it was most likely just an owl. It couldn't hurt her.

She forced herself to be calm, forced her breathing to return to normal, though a prickly chill crept up her arms to her neck. To thwart her increasing fright she once more brought out the medallion from beneath her shirt. She clutched it tightly in one hand while the other hand twisted the cord that tied her cloak about her shoulders.

Another sound crept from the darkness, the rustling of branches and leaves. Vala's heartbeat quickened, and she drew her legs up against her chest.

Elthea Gannabribriel Ithys Kjvali. Just thinking the words made her feel better. The rustling increased, nearer now, and Vala's terror increased with each moment. She began to tremble and silently mouthed the words she had been chanting in her mind. But the sound of movement drew ever nearer, and nearer...then abruptly ceased. For a moment, there was only silence, then a low, throaty growl cut through the darkness.

Vala gasped. A forest cat! It had caught her scent. No! Not hers! The meat in her pack! Panicked, she hurled the bag away, hoping the cat would follow. Instead, the animal issued a yowl of challenge, and broke through the brush separating it from Vala. It was huge, illuminated only by the ghostly light of the moon.

Vala froze in terror as the animal crouched, tail swishing against dead leaves. "Ithys Kjvali," she breathed, then again, as her terror overtook her. "Ithys Kjvali!" Immediately, she reeled, seeming to lose her focus on the woods about her. The ground moved beneath her, and she grabbed for the nearest tree. Her hand closed on air. She fell sideways, throwing out her hands to brace herself, but found nothing substantial to break her fall. With a little squeak of terror, Vala plummeted downward, spiraling into a dark abyss.

Chapter Ten

"**C**ome on, wake up."

The voice was close by, and hauntingly familiar. Vala pried her eyes open to stare at the fuzzy figure hovering over her. She blinked several times, until her vision cleared, then gasped.

"Aric!"

He sighed with relief and sat back. "What are you doing here?" he demanded.

"I'm back?" she breathed. "In Larendalath?"

He grimaced at her. "Yes, you are. Why, I don't know. I thought you didn't want to come here. I thought you didn't want to meet my father. And here you arrive on your own. Why?"

Vala propped herself up on one elbow, her surroundings only just now registering in her foggy mind. She was lying on a large, soft bed, which sported ornate, twisted bedposts, a carved headboard and a beige canopy. A dark wood bureau, several chairs and a desk graced the large room. The stone floor was well padded with various colors of wool rugs, and a fire crackled in the hearth. Vala looked back at Aric.

"Where am I?"

"In my room," he answered. "And you're quite lucky you are. I was just able to snag your entry into Larendalath, otherwise you'd be with my father right now."

"Then this...this is the palace? Your palace?"

He rose from his perch on the side of the bed. "Not my palace," he said tightly. "My father's. It will never be mine."

Vala frowned, remembering his words to Severrani about being a bastard prince. She decided now was not the time to ask him for details of the relationship. "How did I get here? I--I was in the woods."

Aric shrugged, obviously annoyed. "What woods?"

"The woods outside of..." She stopped. She hadn't even asked Tholian what the name of the port village was. "I--I just came across the water from Gannabrina."

"Gannabrina? What were you doing there? How did you get there?"

Vala hesitated, then lay back on the bed with a heavy sigh. "I really don't know, Aric. I was..." She drew a deep breath. "My homecoming didn't go as planned."

"What does that mean?"

"It means that I was imprisoned and convicted of murder by the very people whom I once called neighbor!" Vala retorted, sitting up so quickly it made her head spin.

Aric cringed. "I see."

"That's all you can say? 'I see'?" Vala cried.

"Well, it's not as if it's my fault!" Aric replied, spinning away from her. "I'm not the one who made you a fae. You'll have to level that accusation at Gannabribriel."

"He's dead!" Vala snapped. "The villagers killed him, just as they planned to kill me."

Aric whirled toward her, his face ashen. "They were going to kill you?"

The words only now seemed to hit her, and she sagged against the bedpost, clinging to it. "Yes," she whispered. "They were going to burn me."

"That's disgusting," Aric said. "Why do humans do such atrocious things to each other? To us?"

"I don't know, Aric," Vala replied. "But it's not all humans. Those in Gannabrina aren't like that. They practically worship the fae. I have never been treated so kindly, or with so much love and respect. Why did Severrani leave there?"

Aric hesitated. "How do you know he was from Gannabrina?"

"Because I spoke with an elderly woman there. She was fae actually. She remembered the stories about Gannabribriel, that he had a son named Severrani. I also know that his father, Gannabribriel, was the High Healer of Kjvali." She suddenly gasped and began to search the rumpled bedclothes.

"Are you looking for this?" Aric held up the medallion.

"Yes!" Vala tried to snatch it away from him, but he moved out of her reach.

"Where did you get this?" he asked.

"From my mother," she answered, getting to her feet. "Give it back to me."

"It doesn't belong to you."

"Gannabribriel left it with my mother, for me. Now, give it back!"

"Do you know why he left it with you?" Aric demanded, staying just out of reach.

"No! Maybe because he saved my life, because he cared about what happened to me, because he knew there would come a day when I would need him."

Aric laughed. "None of the above," he taunted. "Who named you Vala?"

She made another failed attempt to get the medallion. "I suppose my parents did. Why?"

"Do you know what your name means?"

"Does it have to mean anything?"

"It doesn't have to, but it does." Aric danced to the other side of the bed, then leaned forward. "It's fae, our language. Didn't you see the way Severrani reacted when you told him your name? He made me say nothing of it. Told me to keep quiet."

"Why?" Vala shook her head, confused. "Why would it matter?"

"It means 'Chosen One'," Aric said. "Chosen One. I can guess who you were chosen for, Vala. Can you?"

Vala stared at him in shock. She shook her head. "No."

Aric snorted in disbelief and straightened. "Are you really this dense? Don't you understand yet? Gannabribriel was killed in Strander, your village. Your people killed him, and he cursed you!"

"What?" Vala stared at him. "What makes you think he cursed me?"

Aric reached out to touch the ends of her hair. "It's all white now."

She looked down at his hand, then pulled away from him. "So?"

"You are daft! Gannabribriel ensured that you would repay the debt of life by forfeiting yours. He made you a fae, Vala. Someone else to serve my father! You belong to Reth Etharid, the King of the Faery Realm. You always have!"

Vala averted her gaze, her stomach tumbling wildly. Another thought leapt to the fore, and she looked up at Aric. "The children? Do the fae take the children of Strander because Gannabribriel died there? Are their lives part of the payment?"

"I would suppose," Aric said, his voice now sounding only tired. "You were the last one to live, weren't you?"

She nodded. "But it wasn't a life, Aric. It was a struggle. I had enough protection while my mother and father lived, but once they died..." She rose, although her shoulders sagged with defeat. "He cursed me," she whispered, and sudden tears stung her eyes. "Why? Why would he curse a mere infant?"

Aric shrugged. "It must have been with his dying breath. He must have struck out at the nearest thing. You." He paused a moment, then edged closer to her. "Do you want to know the truth? The absolute truth?"

She turned to him. "Of course I do. Do you know it?"

"No, not me. This does." He held out the medallion. "Take it. Read the story in the stone."

"The story?"

"Yes, it's said that the bearer's story is hidden in the stone. Why don't you find out how the Elthea died? Then you'll know for sure." He looked her in the eye. "We'll both know."

Vala eyed the medallion in his hand, then slowly reached for it, half-afraid he would snatch it back. But he didn't, and her fingers closed around the smooth metal. She drew it close and stared into the red depths of the inset stone.

"How does it show the story?" she asked.

"I really don't know. I couldn't get it to work. But it might for you since you've had it with you all of this time. Just ask it."

She frowned, looking back at the stone. She sank down on the edge of the bed. "All right. Tell me the story of Gannabribriel," she said.

Nothing happened, and she began to wonder if Aric was just making it up, to see if humans really were as gullible as Severrani claimed.

"Ask it what became of Elthea Gannabribriel," Aric suggested, climbing onto the bed to view the medallion over her shoulder. He seemed as eager to learn the truth as she was.

She did as he said, then gasped as colors suddenly began to swirl and change. She was tempted to let go of the medallion, but found she could not. It was as if her hand were frozen in place, her gaze locked on the stone.

Slowly, an image began to form in the stone's middle. A small room appeared that was achingly familiar.

"That's my cottage," she murmured. "And that! Oh, by the Saints! That's my mother!"

A soft sob escaped her as she watched the beautiful young woman bend to minister to someone laid out on a cot. It was apparent from the amount of blood staining the head wrap, that there could not be much life left in the wounded. Vala stared in amazement, as the vision seemed to enlarge, drawing her closer and closer, until the face of the wounded man became visible.

"And that," Aric whispered, "is Gannabribriel."

"Then he was with my mother when he died?"

"Apparently so. And I expect that was when he cursed your name and ensured that you would one day return to the fae." He leaned closer. "Who's that?"

Vala peered into the stone. The image had shifted again, this time moving outside the cottage. A man lurked outside in the darkness, though he was nothing more than a shadow. She shrugged. "I don't know."

"Ask the stone to clarify it for you," Aric encouraged.

Vala did as he suggested, then gasped aloud as another image rapidly swirled into view. She and Aric stared at the stone, watching Gannabribriel as he was brutally attacked by another man, struck over and over with a heavy cane, wielded by none other than Odig. Vala flung the medallion to the bed and leapt up. She felt each blow as if it had been delivered on her own body, had come down to pummel her own skull. Pain tore through her, and she collapsed on the bed, chilled and trembling, sick, clutching at her head in agony.

Aric stared at her in outright shock. "Vala!" He shook her, his eyes large. "Vala!" He spun. "I have to get someone! I have to find Severrani."

"No!" Her retort was crisp, filled with panic, and she reached out to grab him by the arm. "No! You can't!"

"But --"

"No! Please!" She pushed to a sitting position, her head reeling. "I have to go. I have to get out of here before Severrani finds out what happened."

"What do you mean?"

"That man," Vala managed. "That man who killed Gannabribriel...that was my uncle. I recognized the cane. He used to hit me with it." She struggled to her feet. "I have to get out of here. I have to go."

Aric sat back, slack-jawed. "Your uncle killed Gannabribriel?" He shook his head, then picked up the medallion. "No wonder he cursed you."

The words drove deep into Vala's heart. "It wasn't my fault," she whispered. "It was my uncle, not me."

"Still, to beat someone like that, as if he were no more than an animal..." Aric sank onto the bed beside Vala. "No wonder Severrani hates you!"

Tears flooded Vala's eyes, and she backed away from Aric. "I don't deserve this! Gannabribriel's death wasn't my fault. My uncle isn't right in the mind anymore. He hasn't been since I was a child. He...he used to hit me...and he...he did..." She couldn't bring herself to speak further of her uncle's abuses. She had tried to put them out of her mind, had buried the horror deep. Now, it threatened to surface, to reclaim her. She wouldn't let it. Not now. She forced her thoughts back to Gannabribriel and the vision in the medallion. "My mother...she cared for him. She probably tried to heal his wounds, save him. Doesn't that count for something? I shouldn't have to answer for crimes I did not commit. Aric, please help me! I don't want to belong to your father. I want to go back to Gannabrina. Help me, please."

Aric flinched, then heaved a deep sigh. For a moment, heavy silence filled the space between them.

"Even if you do return to the human world, you will always been viewed as a fae. You've seen how un-accepting Lareriveth is of such."

"But Gannabrina..."

"I can't get you back to Gannabrina. You'll have to do that on your own."

"Then...you'll help me?"

He paused, his gaze on hers. "I probably shouldn't. I'm probably interfering in something that was preordained or something."

"But...?"

"But, to be honest, Vala, I don't think anyone deserves to be a slave to my father, not you or anyone else, no matter what they did."

Vala cringed at the accusation, but did not argue it further. If Aric was willing to help her, she wasn't about to alienate him now. "But what of your father? Won't he take out his anger on you?"

Aric shrugged, although he trembled. "Maybe not. He's recently found a new plaything, someone to keep him amused for the time being. I don't think he knows you're here, and he's already...talked with me about how displeased he was that I let you escape."

Vala heard more there then Aric said. She wondered just how the Reth had 'talked' to Aric. She skipped over the pain-ridden words. "A new plaything?"

"Yes, another human who came into our world. I have to say, she's quite pretty, and seems very nice. It's too bad she has to suffer to him and his whims."

Vala frowned. "Do humans enter your world often then?"

"No. But she got into Talede and...Severrani brought her over. I think he was intending to use her to placate my father so he wouldn't be so upset." He grimaced. "It didn't work."

Vala easily heard the lie behind the words. She doubted very much that it was Severrani who had brought the human over. It would make much more sense that Aric had, as a way of trying to ease his father's anger. Yet, from what Aric had said, the peace offering hadn't worked. Vala scrutinized him for any signs of abuse but saw nothing. She supposed that the Reth could have used magic, though. The very thought sent chills up her spine. Aric's willingness to help her get back to her own world had only created more problems. She never should have left. "Where was this woman from?" she asked absently.

"Why?"

Vala shrugged. "I'm just curious." A sudden thought struck her, and alarm tore through her. "Was she from Strander perhaps?" Aric nodded, and Vala's pulse quickened. "What does she look like?"

"Why?"

"I just want to know. What does she look like?"

"She's slender, about my height, with dark hair and eyes." He paused, his brow furrowing in thought. "Sad eyes, like she's grieving over something. I...I think it might have been her baby that I was supposed to take in the meadow. That's where I...I mean, Severrani found her. In the meadow." For the first time his voice held true remorse, as if he, himself, didn't like what he had probably done.

Vala caught her breath. "Do you know her name?" she whispered.

Aric paused, his brow furrowing as if he were searching his memory. "Yes, I think it's Wanda or something like that."

"Lawanda," Vala breathed, and got to her feet, holding to the bedpost for support. "She's my friend. She came here looking for me. Her husband told me that the fae had taken her, but I didn't really believe him." She gripped his arm. "Aric, can you help me get her back to the other side?"

Aric blanched. "Why?"

"Because she doesn't belong here. Maybe I do, but not her. Please, Aric, please help me."

He hesitated, walking away from her. He stopped before the fire, his back to her. "If I do something like that my father will permanently disown me, or..." He trembled, then shook his head as if shrugging away other thoughts. "It's bad enough that he...ignores me, but to be banished..."

"Then tell me how I can do this myself," Vala pleaded. "I promised her husband that I would return her to him. He has lost much, Aric. Three children, now his wife. He will die of loneliness and grief if she does not return. And I promised him. Please, help me."

Aric was silent for a moment, then slowly he turned to face her. "Severrani's mother died of heartbreak," he whispered. "Perhaps this is only continued payment for that death."

Irritation swept through Vala. "Payment has been made a hundred times over. No child has lived in that village for nineteen years. I am the one who was cursed. And the payment should have rested only with me. I am the cause for all of this grief. Let me be the one who ends it. Please, Aric, please help me."

Aric was quiet for a long time. Vala could see the internal struggle reflected in his eyes. Slowly, he nodded. "All right, I'll help you. But you may be expected to take Lawanda's place with my father."

"Then I shall do so," she said, though her heart ached. What did it matter? If Aric was correct, Severrani hated her anyway. Besides, what would he want with a human? And a tainted human at that? While she knew that what had happened to her was not her fault, it didn't change the fact that she was no longer pure. Perhaps a human man could overlook that, but she didn't know about a fae. Besides, there was a certain amount of sadistic pleasure in knowing that the Reth would be getting spoiled goods. She pushed the thought aside, determined to concentrate on getting Lawanda safely home. "When can we search for her?"

"Now, I guess," Aric replied. "It's as good a time as any. In fact, maybe the best time. The Concubine Chambers have no doubt been closed up for the night. Come on."

Vala followed him from the room into a long hallway. The opulence astounded her. The polished wooden walls gleamed, reflecting the oil lamps that had been dimmed for the evening. Thick, multi-colored carpets lined the hall, softening steps and muffling sounds. Small, marble-topped tables stood in several places along the walls, each holding some trinket or ornament of either cut crystal or shining gold. Aric ignored all, obviously used to such richness, but Vala drank in the beauty surrounding her. So intent was she on the decor she nearly collided with Aric when he stopped to peer around the corner.

"All right," Aric whispered. "The guards have closed the Concubine Chambers."

"Then how shall we get in?" Vala asked.

Aric tossed her a grin and held up a large key, taken from his pocket. "Not everything is done by magic," he told her.

Vala wanted to ask him why he had a key to the Concubines' Chamber, but Aric had already crept down the hallway. Vala followed, her heart pounding so hard it hurt. He stopped before a large, ornately carved wooden door and fitted the key in the lock. It turned silently, and he pushed the massive door open only enough to allow himself and Vala to slip through.

Oil lamps glowed in a large room that was filled with cushions and lounging cots. Huge windows opened onto a garden, where several fountains sparkled in the flames of strategically placed torches. Vala could see a few of the women seated at a table, most likely enjoying the warm night air and star-studded sky. They looked up in surprise as Aric shut the door quietly behind him.

"Prince Aric!"

The voice startled Vala, and she whirled. A tall, slender woman stood before her, wearing only a silk dressing gown that clung suggestively to her ample curves. Her long, red locks were loosely curled about creamy white shoulders, and she twisted one tendril coyly as she addressed Aric.

"Have you finally come looking, my little prince?" she asked, a trace of a smile on her red lips. "Is it time for you to become a man?"

Aric flushed, darted a quick glance at Vala and took a step backward. "N--no," he returned. "I--I was only looking for someone."

"Well, which is it, then? You have or have not come looking?"

"I didn't come looking for...for..." Aric swallowed hard, then drew himself up indignantly. "I am looking for the new woman, Lawanda. Where is she?"

"Oh, so your tastes run to the dark and mysterious?" the woman teased.

"Stop it!" Aric snapped. "Just tell me where she is."

The woman glanced at Vala. "Is this your woman, Aric? A fae?"

"I'm--"

"Yes!" Aric interrupted Vala's retort. "She is my woman. But she seeks a lady servant. I thought that new girl would be a good choice."

The woman hesitated, then flipped her hair over her shoulders, obviously disappointed, and sank down on a cushion. "She isn't here tonight."

Vala caught her breath and clutched at Aric's arm. He shot her a quick glance, then again looked at the woman.

"Is she with my father, then?"

"No, she is with Severrani," the woman replied.

Vala couldn't stop the pain that raced through her at the words. She straightened, determined not to let it show. Aric seemed nonplussed about the information. In fact, he seemed almost relieved. He turned toward the door.

"Thank you," he said quietly, then opened the door and peeked into the hallway. After a moment, he pulled Vala outside, shut the door and relocked it before pocketing the key.

"Why do they have to be locked in there?" Vala asked, irritated.

Aric looked at her in surprise. "For their protection, of course. They are all very beautiful women. There are many who would like to take liberties with them, but they belong to my father. Come on."

His words, with their casual acceptance of his father's ownership of the women, grated on her, and she gave the locked door one last glance, before following Aric down the wide hallway.

"Where are we going now?" she asked.

"To the Healer's Chamber, of course," he replied.

"No!" she cried, pulling him to a stop. "No, we can't go there. I--I mean, if Severrani is...well, if he and Lawanda are..." She closed her eyes, not sure what she really wanted to say. Just the thought of the fae bedding her friend, a married woman, sent pure rage through Vala. She could think of nothing she would like better than to intrude on them and watch him wallow in embarrassment. On the other hand, she didn't want to walk in on them at all, to see them together in that fashion.

Aric looked at her with obvious amusement. "Oh! I see. You thought Severrani had taken your friend to..." He broke off with a quiet chuckle.

Vala flamed red, her irritation increasing by the moment. "Well, hasn't he?"

Aric shook his head. "Severrani has never visited the concubines. Not that he couldn't as the High Healer, but he never has. There are rumors he has a love back in Gannabrina." He stopped outside another door. "You wait here. Let me see if he's in there."

"No!" Vala gripped his arm in panic. "What if someone comes down the hall? What am I supposed to do?"

"No one will. It's late. Don't humans sleep at night?" Aric opened the door to the Healer's Chamber and slipped inside.

Vala pressed against the wall, her breath hard and fast. Only now did Aric's words register. So, Severrani had a lover in Gannabrina. No wonder he longed for the place. Still, he had said he would never go back. Had he been jilted? Was that the reason for his anger when speaking of Gannabrina?

Her gaze darted the length of the hallway. She was sure there was movement at the far end, and she sucked in her breath, visions of weapon-bearing men dancing through her mind. Aric chose that moment to reach through the open door to take her arm. Vala let out a little squeal of alarm. He clamped one hand over her mouth and yanked her inside the room.

"What are you trying to do? Wake the whole palace?" he snapped.

Vala wriggled away from his grasp. "You startled me!"

He shook his head and motioned her to follow. She did so, trying to calm the pounding of her heart. Aric halted outside a doorway.

"She'll be in there," he whispered.

Vala swallowed hard and followed him into the dark room. They walked slowly, silently. Vala kept expecting to bump into something and so stayed as close to Aric as she could by taking hold of his tunic sleeve. They had gone a number of paces when both were stopped cold by a quiet voice that came out of the darkness.

"I've been waiting for you," Severrani said.

Chapter Eleven

Vala watched the fae pace slowly in front of her and Aric. His lean face was set in a scowl, his eyes now a clear blue that reflected the pale color of the walls about him. Lamps, which had suddenly sprang to light, bathed the large room in a subtle glow. Lawanda lay on a healer's cot, covered with a blanket, her eyes closed in some sort of spell-induced sleep. Vala's gaze continually moved from Severrani to Lawanda and back.

Aric stood beside her, shifting uncomfortably and watching Severrani. Finally, the fae stopped before him.

"And I should tell your father what?" he asked.

"Do you have to tell him anything?" Aric mumbled.

"I should not mention the fact that you intercepted a human entering our land? That you then hid the human in your quarters before taking her to the Concubine Chambers, which you know is strictly off-limits for any humans other than the ones housed there? That you brought this woman," he gestured at Lawanda, "to Larendalath as a replacement for Vala."

Vala felt her pulse quicken, her senses tingle at the fact that he had once again said her name out loud. Embarrassed, she drew a long, slow breath.

Aric's gaze shot to her, and a flush spread over his cheeks, but he said nothing about the accusations Severrani had leveled at him. Instead, he turned again to the fae. "H--how do you know all of that?" Aric asked.

Severrani sighed and sat down in one of the richly upholstered chairs. His gaze moved from Aric to Vala, where it remained. "Because," he said quietly, "I have been watching you since our return here."

"Why?" he asked.

He seemed surprised by the question and momentarily at a loss for words. He got up again and went to Lawanda's bedside, where he stood with his back to Vala and Aric. "It is my job," he said softly, pain in the words.

"Your job?" Aric echoed dully. "Then you...you saw everything? Why didn't you stop me from bringing Lawanda here?"

Severrani stiffened. "Perhaps I thought along the same lines as you did, Aric. I also wished to appease your father."

Aric snorted, and turned away. "It didn't work, did it? What was the use? He still..." He stopped, his gaze again going to Vala, and he shook his head.

She winced involuntarily, feeling his pain, then looked at Lawanda. "What's wrong with her?" she asked.

"Nothing," Severrani replied quietly.

"Nothing?" Aric echoed. "Then why is she here instead of in the Concubine Chambers?"

Severrani turned to face him. "That is not your concern. Do you realize what I must also face, Aric?"

"No," Aric admitted. "Not really."

A sad smile touched at the fae's lips. "I allowed you to escape with Vala. I allowed you to bring another human to Larendalath. I was the one who made sure your father did not sense your use of magic to breach the transportation spell when Vala returned. I have not informed your father of her arrival, nor have I given him a good reason for Lawanda to be here. He will be expecting answers to all, Aric, and I have none."

Aric sank into a chair, his shoulders sagging. "I'm sorry," he whispered, then added. "I thought I did quite well with the magic, actually."

Severrani huffed out an exasperated breath, but complained no further.

Vala chewed on the inside of her lip, wondering if she should voice her thoughts. Finally, she decided she had no choice.

"Lawanda is married," she said firmly. "Her husband misses her desperately. He wants her back."

"And you found this out how?" Severrani asked.

"I went back to my village."

"And how were you received?"

Vala paused. "I wasn't," she said tightly. "I was...I was bound and imprisoned. They condemned me to death, by fire. They blame me for all of the deaths in the last nineteen years." She tipped her head, and regarded him thoughtfully. "But, then, you knew how I had been received, didn't you?"

Severrani said nothing, but Vala could tell by the glint in his eyes that he did know of her ordeal. And hadn't bothered to help her. Anger and hurt rushed through her.

"Tyrs released me," she said.

"Tyrs?"

"Lawanda's husband. He thought I could come here and get her back for him." She looked up into the clear blue of Severrani's eyes. "Can I?"

"She said she would take Lawanda's place in the Concubine Chambers," Aric put in.

Severrani's gaze shot to Aric, then back to Vala. "Is this what you want?"

"No! Of course not!" she snapped. "But I would do anything for Lawanda. She was the only one who called me friend. My only regret is that I cannot return her children to her. She has suffered so much. Don't take her away from her life with Tyrs. Please, let her go back. They have already lost many months of their life together. Please, Severrani, if you have it in your power to return Lawanda to Tyrs, please do it." She abruptly gripped Severrani's hand. "Please."

"And you will then go to the Reth? You will become another of his concubines?"

Vala's knees went weak, and she collapsed into the nearest chair. Tears pooled in her eyes, but she nodded. "I don't belong in Strander," she murmured. "I can't go back. And if I must become the Reth's concubine for Lawanda, then I shall."

Severrani was quiet for a long moment, then reached out to wipe away a tear that slid down her cheek. The touch sent a tingle shooting through her, bringing an involuntary gasp. Severrani drew back quickly, a flush creeping over his cheeks. Aric grimaced and looked away.

"Aric," Severrani said, "take Vala back to your quarters. And find her some proper clothing. I will go speak with your father. Perhaps I can persuade him to release Lawanda."

Aric nodded and started toward the door. Vala went to Lawanda. She gently brushed her friend's hair back, then kissed her on the forehead.

"I'm sorry," she whispered. "I'm sorry I couldn't fulfill my promise. Forgive me." She gave Lawanda a last look, then followed Aric from the room.

Instead of heading directly for his quarters, however, Aric pulled her into an alcove several doorways down the hall. She looked at him in question, but he shushed her with a finger to his lips. He seemed to be listening, though Vala heard nothing more than the chiming of a clock somewhere in the palace. After many long moments Aric gripped her hand and once more pulled her after him to the Healer's Chamber. They slipped inside, and Aric closed and bolted the door. Severrani was gone.

"What are you doing?" Vala whispered.

"Father won't let her go. I already know that," Aric replied. "And now you know. I brought her here." He turned away from her. "I'm sorry. I was scared. I panicked. I just..." he took a deep, shuddering breath, then started when Vala touched his arm.

"What did he do to you?" she asked.

He stared at her, as if unable to comprehend the question, then abruptly changed the subject. "If you want to get her home, you'll have to do it yourself."

"Me!" Vala stared at him in shock. "How?"

"I'll tell you the words to say. You just speak them. It's obvious that you have magic. You got here somehow." He dragged her into the smaller room where Lawanda still peacefully slept.

"But how will you wake her?" Vala asked.

"She'll wake the moment you re-enter your own world. Now, get ready. We don't have much time. Severrani--and my father--will sense this use of magic. They'll be hot after me in moments."

"But then you--"

He shushed her with an upraised hand. "Don't worry about me. This is something I want to do. In fact, I wish I could see the look on my father's face when he realizes he's lost not one, but two little playthings. Now, get ready."

Vala swallowed hard, forcing down her disgust at his words. Her fear was another thing, however, and she began to tremble. She didn't want Aric to get into trouble but could see no other way to fulfill her promise to Tyrs. And what of Severrani? Would he also be punished? He had intimated that he was already in enough trouble with the Reth. Would this just add to his offenses? She really didn't want that to happen either. But what choice did she have? She had promised Tyrs. And if she couldn't keep her promise to Lawanda, then she had to keep her promise to Tyrs. The man had risked much to help her. Now it was time to help him. She let out a soft, resigned sigh.

"What do I have to do?"

"Take her hand and repeat what I say, exactly."

"Where will we end up?"

"In the Funeral Meadow, I think," he answered. "Oh, and you'd better give me the medallion."

"Why?"

"Because it's a link to our world. If you have it on, my father can probably track you down. I don't think you want that."

Vala hesitated, then slowly removed the medallion. She stared at the red stone. The medallion had been with her since birth. It provided a comfort that she couldn't identify. Handing it over to Aric didn't seem right. Still, it didn't belong to her. Not really. And as Aric had pointed out, it might well lead the faery king right back to her and Lawanda. Besides, it belonged here, in the Faery Realm. She drew a deep breath and placed the medallion into Aric's outstretched hand. He gripped her hand in his, holding it against the medallion.

"All right," she murmured. "I'm ready."

Aric drew a deep breath, then intoned, "*Ferith salla ithys Strander.*"

Vala repeated his words carefully. Immediately, she was swept up in a whirlwind. It pressed against her from all sides, draining her of energy and sucking the breath from her lungs. She closed her eyes and tightened her grip on Lawanda's hand, determined not to lose her friend in whatever sort of spell this was. A moment later, she was in the Funeral Meadow, in full daylight, staring into Tyrs' shocked face.

Tyrs let out a small gasp of astonishment just as Lawanda opened her eyes and sat up. Tyrs let out a strangled sob, and grabbed his wife in a fierce hug. Lawanda seemed groggy, unable to focus on him or her surroundings. But Tyrs looked at Vala, his eyes swimming with tears. "You have done as I asked," he whispered, then reached out to clench her hand. "My thanks, Vala, my thanks."

She managed a smile, wondering what his attitude would have been had she not been able to return Lawanda. She touched her friend's arm gently, drawing her attention.

Lawanda whirled to face her. "Vala!" Her eyes cleared, suddenly alert. "Where were you? Where have you been? Where did you come from?" She looked around, puzzled, then turned to Tyrs as if for an answer.

Vala thought quickly. "You came with Tyrs to visit your child's burial site. You fainted. That's all."

Lawanda frowned, obviously still confused, then touched lightly at Vala's white hair. "What happened to you? Where have you been?"

Vala hesitated, her gaze darting to Tyrs. But he seemed unwilling to do more than hold his wife. Vala shrugged. "Away. I've been away. Just visiting other parts of our country. That's all."

"But...your hair. It's gone white."

"She's fae," Tyrs mumbled.

Vala stiffened, but Lawanda shook her head. "The sun did this, nothing more."

"The sun?" Tyrs asked, his brow furrowed with confusion.

"Yes," Lawanda answered. "The sun can make hair go white, just as it bleaches out the linens I make."

"But, Lawanda," Tyrs protested, "she went to the Faery Realm and brought you back. She couldn't do that if she were not fae."

Lawanda frowned at him, obviously confused. "What are you talking about?"

He stroked her cheek. "You have been gone for over three months, Lawanda."

Lawanda stared at him, as if trying to make sense of his words. "Three months? But I only just came here! What nonsense do you speak?"

"It is true," Tyrs said. "Tell her, Vala."

Vala sighed. "I don't know how, but it seems to be true. Time moves at a different pace in the Faery Realm." She paused. "Do you remember anything of your stay there?"

Lawanda shook her head. "Nothing. I remember only coming to this meadow to look for you." Tears slid down her cheeks. "I was so afraid for you, Vala. I heard about your uncle. They said you attacked him, then fled the village."

Vala gasped. "I did not attack him! He attacked me!"

Tyrs let out a little snort, then flushed when Lawanda turned condescending eyes his way. "If he attacked you, Vala, then you fought back. We found him unconscious behind the pub."

Lawanda frowned, then shook her head. "Good for you, Vala. It's about time you returned some of his evil to him. He's a hateful, spiteful old man."

Vala stared at her in astonishment, finding no words. Lawanda continued, her voice soft and reassuring.

"When you didn't return to the village I feared the worst. I wanted to search for you, but I had no direction. So, I came here and prayed. When the Gods did not answer, I asked the fae for help."

Vala sagged. "And, instead, they took you," she mumbled. "And three months of your life. Oh, Lawanda, I am so sorry, so very sorry."

"And what do you have to be sorry for, Vala?" Lawanda asked softly.

"I...I was unable to find your children, to return them. I failed in my promise to you."

Lawanda managed a shaky smile. "You didn't fail me, Vala. I told you it was impossible. I am just so happy that you're back, that you're not hurt." She took Tyrs' and Vala's hands in hers. "We can go home now."

"No!" Vala cried, pulling away. She surged to her feet. "No, I can't, Lawanda."

"Why not?" Lawanda asked.

"You have to!" Tyrs snapped at the same time, scrambling up. "The elders were not happy that I freed you, but they agreed to allow me time to prove my reasoning. Lawanda is the proof."

"The proof of what?" Vala asked, backing away. "The proof that I am fae? That I went there and brought her back? Speaking for you will ensure my death, Tyrs."

"Death?" Lawanda looked from one to the other. She rose slowly.

"Yes," Vala replied, choking on her sob. "I was accused of being fae, of causing all of the deaths. I was tried and condemned by those very people I once thought of as neighbor, family. My sentence was death by fire."

Lawanda's eyes grew wide and she whirled on her husband. "Is this true?"

He nodded solemnly. "But they were frightened and angry, Lawanda. First the children were dying, then you disappeared shortly after Vala. They thought she had taken you away as well. I'm sure that when they see you are back they will look upon Vala as only Vala, not fae."

True astonishment raced through Vala. She could hear the placating tone in Tyrs' voice, and it sent anger through her. "No, I'll not chance it! I'll not go back. Ever!"

"But, Vala, where will you go?" Lawanda approached her.

Vala backed away, holding out her hands as if to stop her friend. "I don't know, but not back to Strander. I--I don't want to die, Lawanda. I don't deserve to die."

Lawanda sighed, her shoulders sagging. "No, you don't, Vala. But to go off on your own, with no protection, ensures your death. Please, let me help you."

"You can't," Vala told her. "There is only one place for me now." She backed away and quietly re-spoke the words that Aric had told her to say, substituting the word Gannabrina for Strander.

Nothing happened. The meadow still lay around her. She frowned and tried again, this time using the words from the back of the medallion. Still nothing, and her hand flew to her chest. The medallion! Of course! It wasn't her magic, nothing she had done. It was the medallion! It alone had allowed her to access the faery magic. Without it, she was trapped here, in the human world, a place she did not, could not belong to.

A sob of despair escaped her and she sank to her knees in the grass, wondering at her own stupidity in turning over the one link she'd had to the Faery Realm. She supposed that was Aric's doing, his magic. He didn't want her to come back. She wasn't sure if she was grateful or angry. True, she was away from his father, but she was also away from any hope of finding a place to call home. And away from Severrani. That, perhaps, hurt the most.

Lawanda approached and knelt before her. She reached out to stroke Vala's hair. "I can help you, Vala," she insisted. "First, before we return to the village, we'll dye your hair. There's nothing I can do about your eyes, but the villagers are used to those anyway."

"But they burned my things," Vala sobbed. "I have nothing to return to. Everything is gone."

Anger raced through Lawanda's eyes, and she shot a glance at Tyrs, who flushed and looked away.

"You'll always have a place with us," Lawanda said firmly.

Vala looked at Tyrs, saw the suspicion and trepidation in his face. "I'll bring rejection to you and Tyrs," she muttered. "I don't want to do that."

"Nonsense!" Lawanda snapped. "You're a part of my family, Vala. Let no one denounce that." She rose and pulled Vala to her feet. "Tyrs, you'll help. We need to gather some black walnuts. And we'll need some food and water. You look as if you can use both, Vala." She turned to her husband, who still hadn't moved. "Go, quickly! We'll wait here."

Tyrs glanced at Vala, then at Lawanda again. He shook his head in resignation, then turned and hurried from the meadow.

Vala watched him warily. He would bring back the others, she was sure of it. She turned a pleading gaze on her friend. "Lawanda, I..." She stopped, seeing the determination in Lawanda's brown eyes. "You don't have to do this."

"No, I suppose I don't," Lawanda agreed, brushing Vala's hair back from her face. "But I want to. You're my friend, Vala. I love you."

Her words wrapped around Vala's heart, and she leaned into the older woman, feeling at once safe and very frightened.

Chapter Twelve

"I don't understand this," Lawanda said.

Her voice held the exasperation that Vala felt as she stared at the white ends of hair. Lawanda's hands were stained dark brown from the walnuts, yet none of the color would take on Vala's hair, though they had been working at it continuously the entire day. Tyrs sat nearby, watching them but saying little. Now, Vala looked over at him.

"It seems you're right, Tyrs," she said quietly, unable to stop the tears of failure and defeat. "I guess I am fae."

"No, Vala," Lawanda interrupted. "There has to be another answer for this."

"I'm fae! That's the answer! I'm not a human at all. My whole life has been a lie! Just a lie!"

Lawanda rubbed her shoulder in reassurance. "I still don't believe it."

"Then where do you think you were for the past three months?" Tyrs asked, his own anger and frustration apparent. "How do you think Vala was able to go to the Faery Realm so easily? And what about that attack on Odig? She couldn't have taken him on with her size. She had to have used magic! How can you explain all of that?"

"I--I don't know," Lawanda admitted. "But there is an explanation, Tyrs. I've known Vala since she was born. We grew up together. In all of that time, did you ever see her use magic?" Tyrs remained silent, brooding, and Lawanda continued. "If she had magic, Tyrs, don't you think she would have used it to protect herself?"

Vala glanced at Tyrs, to find him watching her. He had a strange look on his face, as if he had never even thought about what his wife had asked. Vala knew the answer. It had been the medallion. As long as she wore it, she was protected. All of those times her uncle had beat her, the time in the woods, she had not been wearing the amulet. She had not been protected. And now? The knowledge that her one source of protection was gone drove terror through her. She started at the sound of movement in the meadow to the north. Tyrs rose slowly, his brow furrowing. Vala immediately stepped away, her heart pounding. They were coming for her! She knew it! Panic tore through her, and she bolted, Lawanda's cry of surprise following her.

Too late she realized the village men had already surrounded the meadow. She rounded a boulder and stumbled to a stop. Hanlick, The Revered, and several dozen men stood in her path. They carried ropes and chains, and at least three of them also held weapons. Hanlick gave her a grim nod.

"We thought we'd find you here," he said, his voice cold. "When Tyrs went running off with that food and such, we thought you'd come back to work more of your evil magic."

Vala backed away, her mind working feverishly on a route of escape. She couldn't let them take her, not again.

"Tyrs!" Hanlick bellowed. "We know you're out there! Show us your wife. Put some truth to your words, else you'll be punished as well."

Vala took another step backward, away from the group, then cried out in pain as something hard and heavy came down on her shoulder. She staggered away, clutching at her arm, trying to register what had happened. Odig stood in the path, brandishing his thick cane, his eyes narrowed with hate.

"Stop it!" Lawanda shrieked, rushing forward. She placed herself between Vala and Odig. "Are you mad?"

"Not me, girl," Odig spat, "But it's clear you have the Faery Sickness."

"I have no such thing!" Lawanda retorted hotly. "This is Vala. She's lived in our village all of her life. How dare you treat her like this!"

The Revered stepped forward, his gaze on Vala, his words for Tyrs. "What say you, Tyrs? You let the demon escape so she could return your wife. Is this indeed your wife or some fae spawn?"

"No!" Tyrs cried, gaining Lawanda's side. "This is my wife! She may have been imprisoned in the Faery Realm, but she is not fae. One need only look at her to see that."

"No, I am not fae," Lawanda agreed. "Nor is Vala. She journeyed to the Faery Realm to rescue me, to bring me back here to my husband, my home."

"And just how was she able to do that?" Hanlick demanded, then answered his own question. "Because she's a fae demon, that's how!"

Some of the men nodded in agreement, and hefted their weapons. The Revered raised a hand, silencing them. "And the children?" he asked. "Where are they? Did you bring them back, too?"

Vala drew a trembling breath, clutching her injured arm. "I saw no children, else I would have brought them back as well."

"Hanlick, look!" Another man approached, carrying the pail holding the black walnut water.

"What is it?" Hanlick asked, peering at the water.

"I'll tell you what it is," Odig boomed. "It's dye, meant to disguise the color of her hair, to make us believe that she is one of us. But watch." He grasped the pail, and poured the cold contents directly over Vala's head.

She gasped as the icy liquid seeped into her clothing, dripped down her face, ran in rivulets down both arms. Though her clothing instantly took the stain, nowhere did it leave a mark on her skin. The villagers fell back a step, murmuring amongst themselves. Vala wiped the black water from her face.

"That means nothing!" Lawanda snapped. "I simply didn't make it right."

Odig dropped the pail, reached and grabbed Lawanda by both wrists, holding her arms high, showing her stained hands to all. "It looks like it works fine," he said, "on those who are human."

Lawanda wrested away from him and moved closer to Vala. Tyrs started toward her, then stopped as a low rumble crept over the darkening meadow. The villagers turned as one, and Vala's heart began to pound. She started when Lawanda gripped her by the wrist.

"Do you hear them?" she asked the villagers. "The wolves are coming out, brought by Vala's silent plea for help."

Vala gasped, her gaze flying to Lawanda's face. "N--no," she whispered, completely flustered by the pronouncement. Perhaps she was wrong, perhaps Lawanda had sided with the others. She tried to pull her arm away, but Lawanda only tightened her hold and continued.

"If you don't allow us to leave the meadow, the wolves will attack, their fury driven by your act of violence against she whom they call mistress."

The Revered swung his head around to study Lawanda, his face pale. "You? You wish to leave as well? Go with the fae?" he asked.

"Yes," Lawanda replied calmly. "For I have been enslaved by the fae. I cannot go against her bidding. To do so will bring death and destruction upon all of you, you whom I call family. Please, heed my words. Leave this meadow, quickly, before it's too late."

The people backed away as the growls intensified. Vala stared at Lawanda, wondering if her senses had left her completely. Tyrs' face was confused and full of fear.

The Revered looked to Tyrs. "And you, has this demon also enslaved you? Must you go along?"

"No," Lawanda interrupted. "The fae have no interest in him. My return was only at my plea to save my husband's honor. Now that you know why he allowed Vala to escape, you can forgive him for his rash act. It was done out of love for me, nothing more."

The growls of the wolves grew louder. A sudden howl went up, startling the villagers into action. Most of them hurried away, back toward the village and safety. Only the Revered, Hanlick and Odig remained.

"It is as I told you," Odig raged. "She possesses and kills. Run, Tyrs, run for your life. It is too late for Lawanda. Her soul has been taken by the faeries. Her time in the Faery Realm has drained her of her human side. You must kill the fae, Tyrs. Kill her, and your wife will be free."

The Revered shot a glance at Odig, then turned to Tyrs. "What say you? Will you return to the village, all accusations dropped? Or will you choose to journey with this shell of your wife?"

Tyrs paled. "I--I wish to be with Lawanda."

"Then so be it," the Revered said. "We will pray for your soul, Tyrs, and for your safe return." He looked at Vala, even as the wolf's howl came again. "If there is any decency or compassion in the fae, you will release Lawanda from this spell you have cast."

Vala winced as Lawanda's fingernails dug into her flesh, silencing any protests.

The Revered huffed out an angry breath, then motioned for the others to follow him from the meadow. Hanlick went eagerly, clanking the chains together to keep the wolves at bay. Odig glared at Vala.

"Your days are numbered, fae! Mark my words," he snarled, then spat on the ground beside her feet before hobbling after the others.

Vala watched them go, then turned to Lawanda. "Lawanda, I..."

Lawanda shushed her. "They're fools. I am not about to stand by and watch them condemn an innocent person."

"But I'm not innocent!" Vala cried. She pulled her arm away from Lawanda's grip and spun away from her. "I should have died at birth. I shouldn't even be here right now."

"Nonsense," Lawanda said, her voice firm, resolved. "Tyrs, fetch our supplies, please. We're leaving."

"You can't do this!" Vala told her. "This is your home, your life is here."

Lawanda smiled at her and placed one hand on her wet shoulder. "It *was* my life. It's time to move on. I'll not associate myself with people who refuse to see the truth, who will condemn someone just because they are different." She fingered Vala's wet tunic. "I wish I had something dry for you to change into. You'll catch a chill in these."

"It doesn't matter," Vala murmured as Tyrs rejoined them. She looked at the man. "Talk to her, Tyrs. Make her see how mad this is."

Tyrs was quiet a long moment, then a sudden smile touched at his lips. "She's a stubborn one, she is. Once she's set her mind to something there's no changing it. That's why I love her so." He draped one arm about his wife's shoulders, leaned forward and kissed her cheek gently. "I believe you, Vala," he said quietly. "If I didn't before, I do now."

"Why? Why now?"

He shrugged. "It's as Lawanda said. If you were truly fae you would have used your magic. You wouldn't have allowed your uncle to strike you. And you wouldn't be so concerned about Lawanda and me. That's not the way of the fae. But it is the way of Vala, my friend." He paused. "I'm sorry it took me so long to see things as they are. I'm as big a fool as the others. Vala, please accept my apologies. I shouldn't have sent you away, I shouldn't have allowed the others to burn your things. My only excuse is the loss of child and my grief. I'm sorry."

Vala stared at him, astonished. Lawanda smiled, and linked her arm through Tyrs'. "And that's why I love him. He can admit his mistakes. He can apologize. There aren't many men who can do that."

Tyrs shot her an amused glance, then started as movement came again through the grasses. "We need to move on. Quickly."

Vala allowed herself to be guided away, her heart swelling with love for these two who would risk so much for her.

Vala hugged her legs tight against her chest, resting her chin atop her knees. The trio had walked until it became too dark to see. Now, Tyrs and Lawanda slept on the other side of a small fire, curled up together under a thick blanket. The night was cold and Vala was thankful that Tyrs had managed to secure what he had in the way of supplies. She reached up to draw her own blanket tighter, though it was doing little to stay the chill that coursed through her entire body. Her clothes were still damp but there had been nothing else to change into. Still, the chill she experienced had less to do with her wet clothes, the cold night or the bracing wind that blew across the meadows, than it did with her fear.

She was sure that the villagers would come after them. At least, she was sure her uncle would. And he would have no shortage of followers. He was an elder of the village. What he said, others most often believed. Vala was amazed that she had survived the number of years she had without being hauled away and hung from the nearest tree. Now, with her white hair and proven visits to the Faery Realm, she was positive a tree had already been readied for her.

She shivered and rose, her gaze on Lawanda and Tyrs. How could she stay with them? How could she endanger their lives? They could return to Strander, carry on, maybe even... Vala sighed, her heart heavy with grief. Start a family? No, not until the curse was lifted. With Gannabribriel dead, that task would rest on Severrani. But would he? Would his anger and grief allow him to forgive the villagers?

Tears stung her eyes, and she tilted her head back to stare at the thin sliver of moon that was visible in the dark sky. She had to leave Lawanda and Tyrs, had to force them to return to Strander without her. Then what? How would she get back to the Faery Realm without the medallion? Had Aric known that by taking it from her he was condemning her to a life on the run? Or worse, death? She shook the unpleasant thought aside.

She couldn't figure Aric out. One moment he was antagonizing her, the next he was helping her. He had seemed to genuinely want to get her away from his father, from a life of sexual servitude to the Reth. On the other hand, he hadn't really thought what throwing her, unprotected, back into her own world might cause. She surmised that he didn't think much on his actions. Then again, she hadn't been too quick on her feet either when her main goal was how to stay from under Odig's cane. Perhaps Aric was in that same spot with his own father. Despite Severrani's denial of such, Vala was sure that the Reth punished Aric severely for his mistakes. Maybe not physically, maybe he used magic, but the results would be the same. Aric would be in constant fear.

She sighed and looked west. She wondered how far it was to the port city where Tholian's boat had docked. She wondered if he was still there. A small pang pricked her heart, and she turned back to her friends. She had to leave them and there was no better time than now. She wanted to get back to

Gannabrina, to be somewhere she at least felt safe. She just had to figure out how to accomplish that.

She rose quietly, and crept away, taking nothing but the blanket she wore. She would not deprive Lawanda and Tyrs of food or water, things she could do without, things she could possibly find on her travels.

Fatigue claimed her as the first traces of sunlight crept into the sky. She sagged onto a boulder, watching the sun fire the sky alive with brilliant hues of pink, orange and yellow. It was beautiful, and a sudden thought touched her mind. She wondered what color Severrani's eyes would be in witness to this grand spectacle of nature. She tried to think of them sporting all of the colors in the sunrise, but could not.

Although thoughts of the fae tortured her heart, she was too tired to drive them away. She looked at the finger bitten by the sandshrew. It seemed so very long ago now, yet she could still remember Severrani's touch as he cared for the wound. By the Saints, how she missed him!

"What foolishness!" she said out loud. "He has no feelings for me. He answers only to the Reth. Gods!"

She pushed herself to her feet, and staggered on. The day passed in silence, broken only by the wind periodically spiraling through the treetops. She saw no life, human or otherwise, and finally, as daylight eroded, she stopped. Her throat ached for water, yet she had seen no signs of a stream or river. Using her last bit of strength, she dragged herself into a brush shelter, pulled her blanket close and tried to sleep. Her dreams invited Severrani and Gannabribriel, her mother and father, the village that was no longer hers.

They alternated between soft, pleasant memories and harsher ones. She woke to bellows of anger and hysteria.

Voices echoed in the meadow and the copse of trees. Vala crawled from her hiding place to peer outward through narrowed eyes. It was not yet light, and the trees moved like black ghosts in the brisk morning breeze. For a moment there was silence, then the voices came again, excited and a little wary. She could just make out the words.

"There! Over there! Cut him off!"

"I see him! We'll get the demon!"

Vala's heart leapt in horror. Demon? Him? She threw her blanket aside and scrambled to her feet.

"Watch out!" the voices called. "He might have magic!"

Vala drew a quick breath, straining her ears toward the sounds, trying to ascertain a direction. Breaking branches, pounding of feet came from her right; and she whirled, then darted into the forest before her. A strange sense guided her footsteps, told her where to run, where to turn. Her breathing was hard and fast, burning her throat and chest, cramping her sides. Finally, she saw him, and she slid to a stop with a gasp of shock.

Aric!

He leaned against a tree, clutching at his side with one arm while supporting himself with the other. Even from this distance Vala could see the pain etched on his lean face. A face that had been bruised and battered, that still bore dried blood on swollen lips. She could also hear his pursuers closing in. She rushed forward, startling him into action. He raised his arms toward her, fists balled as if to strike her, then suddenly went limp as their gazes met.

"Can you climb?" Vala whispered frantically.

Aric was pale, sweating, but he nodded, looking up at the tree they stood under. With the agility of a squirrel, Vala scampered upward, waiting impatiently for him to follow. He did so, more slowly and with obvious pain.

She motioned for him to pass by her, then prodded him ever higher into the green foliage. At last he stopped, his breathing ragged and hard, his face contorted with agony.

"No further," he begged.

Vala glanced to the ground, not sure if they were high enough to avoid detection. Reluctantly, she drew him away from the trunk, out onto a thick limb, then wrapped the heavy branches about them both. He sagged against her, his whole body shuddering.

A moment later, his pursuers arrived underneath the tree. Vala held Aric tightly as she, too, began to tremble.

"Where'd he go?" one of the men asked, and Vala recognized the voice as Hanlick's.

"Don't know," another answered. "Probably used his magic to get away."

"Well, he got hit pretty good," a third said. "I don't see how he could have gotten very far, even with magic."

"Let's keep searching. We'll get the demon yet."

Vala waited until she heard the men race off before she turned to Aric.

"What are you doing here?" she whispered.

"Looking for you," he murmured.

"Why?"

Aric grimaced, and shrugged, then moaned in pain.

Vala frowned, confused. "What happened to you? Who hit you?"

"I didn't see them coming. An old man hit me with a big stick or something. I think he broke my ribs."

"A big stick?" She grimaced. "It was most likely a cane. My uncle's cane. But what about your face? Who did that?"

Aric looked at her, avoiding her questions. "Your uncle seems like a nice man. He and my father ought to get together," he said.

"Your father?"

Aric shrugged, turning away but not fast enough to hide the tears that glittered in his eyes. Vala took his arm.

"What does your father have to do with this?" she asked, although she had guessed the answer.

Aric sighed. "He wasn't all that pleased when he found out that I let you and Lawanda go. We had...words. He forced me to come and get you."

"Words?" Vala's gaze raked over his battered face. "He did this to you?" Aric nodded weakly and Vala's stomach tightened in disgust. "He had no right. It wasn't your fault. I was the one who begged you, who coerced you into sending me back."

Aric snorted. "Right. And I didn't have any say in the matter. Please, Vala, don't accept the entire blame. I wanted you and Lawanda out of Larendalath as badly as you wanted out. I just didn't expect my father to react quite so...violently. I guess he was having a bad day."

"A bad day! Fathers don't beat their children just because they're having a bad day!"

"Mine does."

"Oh, Aric, I'm so sorry," Vala whispered, then stiffened as the men returned. She motioned Aric to be silent, but he had crumpled into a ball.

"He can't be far away," one of the men stated.

"You're right. He'll be looking for Vala," another said quietly. "Find her, we find him."

Vala caught her breath. The Revered! So, he was in on this hunt as well, he who preached love and forgiveness, who spoke of peace and acceptance. A sick feeling tore at Vala. She glanced at Aric.

"Can you get back?" she whispered, her mouth close to his ear.

"Of course," he mumbled. "But I'm not going back."

"You have to! Severrani can help you. Find him. Don't go to your father."

"No," Aric insisted. "I am not going back! I've already gotten Severrani into enough trouble as it is. Father could well put him to death over this. No, I'll just stay here and accept whatever happens."

Vala clenched her jaw in annoyance but remained quiet. She guessed the men below the tree would soon tire and move on. She was not disappointed, although it took longer than she had hoped. By the time they gave up on the search and wandered back toward Strander, Aric was again slouched against her in a half-faint. She shook him alert.

"They're gone," she murmured. "Now, how do you get back to Larendalath?"

He mumbled something unintelligible and Vala sighed, her mind working feverishly. Finally, she tugged at his sleeve, gaining his attention. "Come on, I know where we can go."

He didn't ask any questions but followed her down the tree. Several times he slipped, and it was only Vala's grip that kept him from falling. By the time they reached the ground, her muscles were quivering in protest. Gently, she pulled his arm over her shoulder, then, half-dragging him, she turned her steps west. She didn't know quite what to expect, but she was hoping she would again see the white cliffs and the ocean beyond. She knew she had slipped over the border of the Faery Realm the first time she had fled the meadow. She wasn't sure how she had done it, but she was hoping that with Aric along the gates would again open for her.

They walked slowly, steadily through the forest for most of the morning, and nowhere did Vala see any signs of the cliffs. Finally, she had to stop, to allow Aric a badly needed rest. His face was deathly pale, his blue eyes ringed with dark circles. His breath came fast and shallow, and he moaned as she lowered him carefully to the ground.

"Aric," she murmured, hunkering down before him. "You need to go back. You're hurt. You need help. You could die out here."

"So?" he wheezed and made no attempt to hide his tears. "It's just one more bastard dead, then."

"You keep saying that. What do you mean, bastard?"

"Don't you know what a bastard is?"

"No, not really."

He looked up at her, his eyes so full of pain it made her wince. She took his cold hand in hers and began to rub it gently.

"The Reth is my father," he said softly. "But only by birth, not by love. My mother was one of his concubines. Apparently, not one of his favorites."

"Was?"

"She's most likely dead now. She dared to defy him. He came for her one night. She turned him away because I was ill, and she wanted to be with me. He banished her, sent her away, somewhere in the human world. I don't know where. Probably here, in Lareriveth. That would be his kind of punishment."

"Oh, Aric, I'm so sorry," Vala whispered.

"Not half as sorry as I am. I don't care about Etharid. He's nothing to me. But he wouldn't let me go with her. He said it was because I carried royal blood and he wasn't about to have to pay any form of ransom for me. But I think the real reason is because he wanted to break her heart by separating us. It was just part of his punishment." He rubbed his face, then looked at her again, tears standing in his eyes. "Now do you see why I didn't want you to stay there? Why I risked so much to help you escape? I hate him, Vala. I could never condemn someone I care about to a life with him. And I would do anything to be free of him." He shook his head. "You wouldn't understand."

"I understand more than you think, Aric. We're not so different." She touched his bloodied, swollen lips, his words aching in her heart. He cared about her, about what happened to her. Just the idea sent flutters to her stomach. No one had ever cared for her before except Lawanda. "I just wish you hadn't--" She broke off with a gasp as the ground beneath them suddenly moved. She knew this feeling!

Apparently, so did Aric, and he grabbed her with both hands, digging his fingers into her upper arms.

"No!" he raged. "No, I won't go back!"

Vala cried out as the land heaved. She was thrown backward, slamming hard against the ground, Aric coming atop her. The trees overhead began to spin, their colors mingling, fusing, blending into a green swirl, that flew outward to meet the blue sky beyond.

Aric screamed words that were foreign to her, his face dark with anger. Vala closed her eyes and fought against nausea as the world continued to spin in a blur. Then, unexpectedly, it stopped. She clutched at the ground, digging her fingers into...sand.

Startled, she opened her eyes. Aric threw back his head and roared in fury, then rolled away from her. She sat up slowly, her head still spinning. The crash of the waves washed away Aric's cry, the cold sting of the salt air calmed her turbulent belly.

They were back in Talcde.

Chapter Thirteen

"**A**ric!" The command was sharp.

"Leave me alone!" Aric cried, scrambling to his feet.

Vala looked up. Her stomach tumbled, her breath catching in her throat. Severrani stood on the beach, his handsome face twisted into a mask of anger. He cast her but a quick glance before returning his attention to Aric. The boy had turned his back on the fae to stare out over the ocean.

"Explain yourself!" Severrani demanded.

"There's nothing to explain," Aric shot back.

Severrani glared at him, then strode forward, grabbed his arm and spun the boy to face him. A gasp escaped the Healer, and his blue eyes widened when he saw Aric's battered face. Vala wondered why the nasty bruises and cuts hadn't healed upon re-entry into the Faery Realm.

"Who did this to you?" Severrani demanded.

"Does it matter?" Aric snapped, trying to pull his arm away from the fae's grip.

"Yes! It matters a great deal! Tell me!"

"It wasn't my people!" Vala interrupted, getting to her feet. "At least, not his face. My uncle did hit him, but not his face."

Severrani tossed her a scathing glance, then looked back at Aric. "Who, Aric?"

"My father!" Aric shouted. "All right? My father! The great king of the fae! The wondrous faery king! He hit me! Is that what you wanted to hear, Severrani?" This time he was successful in pulling free, and he stomped to the base of the cliff, where he collapsed.

Severrani stood still, as if frozen by the harsh words. Vala watched him, wondering at the emotions that rolled off the fae like the waves rolling on the shore. He caught her eye and drew a deep breath.

"It's my fault," Vala murmured. "If I hadn't asked him to return Lawanda, none of this would have happened. I'm the one who should have been punished, not him."

"He should not have undertaken the decision himself," Severrani retorted, his tone flat.

"He was only thinking of me. He said that his father wouldn't let Lawanda go. Aric didn't want her, or me, to...to..." She broke off, too disgusted to even say the words. "If you would have helped, perhaps Aric wouldn't have--"

"Silence!" Severrani snapped. "The fact of the matter is, I was trying to help. The Reth had not yet touched your friend. I was keeping her in the Healer's Chambers until I could return her home myself."

"You were?" Aric mumbled. "Why?"

Severrani hesitated, but when he answered his voice was soft. "That is not your concern, Aric."

Aric shrugged and drew his knees up to his chest, then gasped in pain and extended them again. Severrani regarded him with concern.

"You're hurt," he stated, moving toward the boy.

"It's nothing," Aric retorted. "Leave me alone."

Vala couldn't stand to see him in pain any longer. "He may have some broken ribs," she said, wondering again why his injuries hadn't healed themselves.

Aric glared at her but didn't dispute her words. Severrani hunkered down in front of him. After a brief pause, he reached forward to probe gently at Aric's side. Aric yelped and moved away from him.

"Just leave it be," he snapped. "If I'm going to survive in the human world, then I have to get used to pain. That's just the way it is there."

"You are not going to live in the human world, Aric," Severrani told him. "You cannot. No more than Vala can."

"I can," Vala cried. "I'll return to Gannabrina. I'll--"

Severrani whirled on her, his eyes wide, his face ashen. "Gannabrina? You were there?"

"Y--yes." She was caught off-guard by his reaction.

"How?"

"I don't really know how I got there," she admitted. "I was in the Funeral Meadow. I--I was attacked by wolves. I begged for help." Sudden tears stung her eyes, spilled down her cheeks; and she began to tremble as memory returned full and furious. "I called out to you, to Aric, but neither of you answered. I begged for help. The wolves...they were..." She sagged to the sands. "It was due payment, wasn't it? I allowed Lawanda's baby to be taken by the wolves, to suffer to their cruelty. Why should I suffer less?"

"The baby was already dead," Aric said.

The words only served to add more pain to Vala's grief, and she began to sob quietly.

"I--I didn't mean it that way," Aric stammered. "I just meant that the baby didn't suffer."

Vala nodded, understanding, but still swallowed whole by her heartache.

Severrani sighed. "The attack in the meadows was not payment of any sort. Wolves have a tendency to attack, especially when they are hungry." He paused a moment, then added, "I would never suffer anyone to such a cruel fate, no matter what you think of me." He turned back to Aric. "And you cannot hold onto pain and injury as punishment to yourself either."

Aric averted his gaze, his shoulders sagging.

Severrani said nothing more about Gannabrina, although his gaze now rested on the sea. Vala glanced over her shoulder at the water.

"Why did you leave there?" she asked softly. "It's a beautiful place. I have never felt so at peace as I did when I was there."

"You felt that way in Gannabrina?" Severrani asked, his tone wondering.

Vala nodded. "In fact," she said, "I want to go back. It's apparent that I can't live in Lareriveth, nor would I want to. At least, not the way it is now. And I don't want to be in Larendalath either." She couldn't bring herself to say why, that it would be incredibly lonely and painful having him so close and yet so far from her reach.

Severrani lowered himself to a bit of driftwood, as if the strength had been drained from his body. "Aric, please, come here," he said.

"Why?" The boy crouched against the cliff, his face pinched with pain.

Severrani turned to face him. "You have suffered enough. There is no need to continue."

"What do you mean? My ribs?"

"That, and so much more. Come here."

Aric slowly got to his feet and approached the fae. Severrani helped him sit down on the driftwood.

"You can't heal me here," Aric said. "And I'm not going back to Larendalath."

Vala frowned in confusion. Severrani seemed to read her thoughts and answered.

"The Reth has decreed that I shall have no magic in the human world, and very little in the world between. What I possess in the way of magical healing lies only in the Faery Realm."

"I don't understand. When I fell from the cliffs I was hurt, yet when I woke here, I was healed. And the bites and scratches from the wolves were healed when I woke in Gannabrina. Why isn't Aric healed?"

The boy shrugged, then winced. "I can't be. My father stripped that ability from me after he...punished me for defying him. He told me I would have to suffer until I returned both Vala and Lawanda to him."

Severrani stiffened, anger flashing through his blue eyes. "I see. Then we need to get someplace with magic so I can tend to your wounds. Either here, or in Gannabrina."

"Then, you were there?" Vala asked. "In Gannabrina?" She shot him a sidelong glance and forced the next words from her mouth. Her aching need to know the truth overrode her fear of his irritation. "Aric tells me that you have a love in Gannabrina. Don't you miss her?"

Severrani looked at her, obviously startled. "A love? The only love that I have in Gannabrina is for the land itself. And, yes, I do miss it. Very much."

Vala's heart leapt at the words. No lover? No beautiful young fae waiting for him? Vala could scarcely contain her relief. At the same time, she had to remind herself that even if Severrani had no lover waiting for him in Gannabrina, that didn't mean he didn't have feelings for anyone else. Perhaps even someone in Larendalath. That thought dulled Vala's joy, and a heavy sigh escaped her, almost unbidden.

"My mother..." Severrani drew a breath, as if forcing himself to continue. "My mother was a princess of Gannabrina. She was the only heir to the throne. As such, she was not allowed to marry outside of royalty, yet she deeply loved my father. I am a product of that love."

Aric stared at him in obvious shock. "Then you're a bastard as well!"

A grim smile curved Severrani's lips. "Not as well, Aric, for you are no such thing. Your birth is quite legitimate."

"But my mother was only a concubine," Aric argued. "I hardly consider that legitimate."

Severrani looked at him. Tears stood in the blue eyes. "Your mother was royalty, Aric. You are the legitimate heir to the throne. There is no bastard blood in you."

Aric's mouth dropped open in disbelief. "No. My father said..."

"Your father lied."

"Are you sure?" Aric whispered.

"Quite sure. I have safeguarded this secret for most of your life."

"Then who was she? Where is she now?"

Severrani was silent for a long moment, as if considering whether he should go on. When he did, there was a depth of grief in his voice Vala had not yet heard. "She is dead, Aric. She died shortly after your birth, fifteen years ago."

"Then I am the cause of her death?" Aric asked, despair clouding his face.

"No," Severrani answered at once. "The humans are."

Vala caught her breath, backing away. "How so?" she demanded. "I suppose you're going to blame that on me, too."

Severrani looked at her. "You were but a child. You could not have caused her death. Yet, you are linked to it."

"In what way?" Vala asked, her anger rising.

"This is difficult for me to say," Severrani told her. "If I continue I will be breaking a vow of silence that I have sworn to the Reth."

"Then say nothing more!" Aric declared, gripping his arm. "I will not see you punished by my father."

"Yet, it must be said at some point, Aric. I have been by your side for most of your life. I have been sworn to your protection, your upbringing, your discipline. I have abided by your father's wishes all of that time, no matter the lies he may have told you. But now, after this..." He touched gently at Aric's battered face. "I can no longer bear to see you suffer from his touch."

"Then let me go away," Aric begged. "Let me and Vala go back to the human world. We can live there. Or we can go to Gannabrina and live there."

"And what would keep your father from hunting you down?"

"I don't know!" Aric cried, then gasped, doubling over in pain.

Severrani caught at him. "I cannot heal you here. We must return to the palace."

Aric wrested away from him. "No! You may go back if that is what you wish, but I will not! And there is nothing you can do to make me."

Irritation flooded Severrani's face, but it was rapidly replaced by surprise. Vala cried out in alarm as she was once more gripped by magic. Seconds later, she, Aric and Severrani all stood in the Funeral Meadow. Severrani turned on Aric with rage.

"What is the meaning of this?" he demanded.

"I--I didn't mean to bring you here," Aric stammered, true despair showing in his eyes.

"Then why did you? No! How did you?"

For a moment Aric was silent, then he reached into his pocket and drew out the medallion. Severrani's gasp mingled with Vala's.

"Where did you get that?" he breathed.

"From her." Aric stabbed a finger at Vala.

Severrani spun to face her. "And you got it how?" he demanded.

"I--I got it from my mother," she managed. "I--I guess Gannabribriel left it with her."

"Left it?" He spun back to Aric. "Give it to me."

"No." Aric backed away, lifting his chin in defiance. "If I give it to you you'll just take me home, and I told you I'm not going back."

Rage darkened Severrani's eyes, and he advanced on Aric. "Give it to me," he said again, his voice low and cold.

"No!" Aric shouted. "No, I won't! I'm not going back! Ever!" He whirled and bolted, tearing across the meadow and disappearing into the woods beyond.

"Aric!" Vala screamed, starting after him. She was shocked he could even run in his condition, more shocked that he had openly defied Severrani.

The elder fae clenched his jaw in anger, drew his sword, and hastened after Aric, Vala trailing. They didn't have to go far. Aric had run directly into the camp of the men still looking for him.

Hanlick was the first to recover from the surprise of having their prey run straight at them. "It's the demon, returned!" he bellowed. "Get him!"

Vala tossed a quick glance at Severrani, who stood as if stunned by Aric's actions, by the hunting party who came to their feet.

"Go back home! Get Aric out of here!" she ordered, then spun towards the men. "Hanlick! It's me! Vala! If you wish to save your precious village, you'd better move!" She waited just until their attention had swept to her, then she darted back into the meadow, heading toward the village, hoping to draw the men away from Aric. She prayed Severrani would do as she said, and get Aric out of danger. She prayed even harder that he would not resort to violence. It would only make matters worse.

"Vala!"

Lawanda's voice carried over the meadow grasses. She and Tyrs were running toward Vala from one direction, the men from the other. Vala stumbled to a stop, not knowing which way to go. She could not implicate Lawanda again. She wouldn't.

"No, Lawanda!" she screamed, loud enough for the men to hear. "Go back! You're free! I revoke my spell! Go back!"

The men slid to a halt behind her, even as Lawanda and Tyrs reached her, panting.

"Where did you go?" Lawanda cried. "We've been looking for you for hours!"

Vala shook her head, unsure what to say, what to do. Another cry went up from behind the men, and she turned.

"See here, fae," the Revered shouted at her. "See what we've got."

Vala caught her breath as The Revered and Hanlick approached. Aric sagged in Hanlick's grasp. Fresh blood stained his face and tunic. He looked barely able to stand, and rage flew through Vala, her fear forgotten.

"Let him go!" she shrieked. "He has done nothing! Let him go! Severrani!"

"Who's that?" Lawanda asked, pointing at Aric.

"He--he's my friend," Vala stammered. "They can't do this! He hasn't done anything! He came back to find me, to help me. Aric, where's Severrani? Where did you send him?"

"Home!" Aric retorted. "I sent him home!"

Vala sagged in defeat. "Please," she begged the men, "don't hurt him. Please."

"They won't do anything!" Lawanda seethed and stepped toward the men. "Let him go, Hanlick. This whole thing has gotten out of hand. By the Gods! He's only a child. Now let him go!" She spun on The Revered. "You're a man of the Gods. Act like it!"

The Revered glared at her. "The Gods have spoken," he declared. "Let no demon live to harm others."

"He's not a demon! Neither is Vala! Use your eyes, man! Look at them," Lawanda retorted. "If he was a demon, do you think he'd let Hanlick hold him like that? Would he be bleeding and in so much pain he could barely stand? Now, let him go!"

Hanlick looked at Aric, his face registering confusion, but he relaxed his hold on Aric. At once, the boy slid to the ground. Vala started toward him, but was suddenly blocked by Odig's cane. She gasped, her gaze darting to his face. She had not seen him approach. The old man's face was dark with rage, as his gaze flicked over first Aric, then her. He stabbed a finger at Lawanda.

"You speak for one of your own kind, demon!" he said. "It's a ploy. You'll convince us of his innocence, of her innocence, then stand by while they kill us all!"

"Oh, by the Gods!" Tyrs snapped, joining Lawanda. "Hanlick! Bern! You've known Lawanda and me all of our lives. You've known Vala. Will you let such words of hate poison your minds against these two? So, they are different than us. Does that mean we should kill them? And if we do kill them, how does that make us any better than them?"

Bern grimaced and glanced at the other men, then abruptly he took a step to one side. "I'll not be a part of this anymore," he said quietly. "As Lawanda has said, this has gone too far. I'm no murderer."

There was a murmuring amongst the men, and three others silently moved to stand beside Bern. With a muttered oath, Odig raised his heavy cane and brought it down hard against the young man's head. Bern yelped, stumbling backward in shock as blood gushed from a gaping wound. Vala cried out in horror as he crumpled. Completely forgetting that just moments before he had been in pursuit of her, she rushed to his side, and dropped to the ground, her gaze raking over the man. The other men had moved backward, away from Odig, confusion on their faces.

Bern didn't move, but looked up at her through eyes glassy with pain, then tried to smile. "I guess I always knew you weren't fae, Vala," he whispered, then fumbled for her hand. "I...I even considered courting you at one time. Even if no one else does, I like your blue eyes." He shuddered, his own eyes falling shut.

Vala stared down at him, astounded that he would actually voice his feelings in front of all of those gathered, including The Revered.

"Vala!" Aric yelled. "Here! Get away while you can!" He moved slightly, and something flew from his outstretched hand. It landed in the dirt at Vala's side. Odig started forward, but found his way suddenly blocked by Tyrs and two other men. He stopped, obviously unsure what to do. Even The Revered was looking at him as a stranger. He glowered at them all, then abruptly turned and strode away.

Vala immediately returned her attention to Bern. She snatched up the medallion, but instead of speaking the words that would take her away, she turned at once to Bern. Without a conscious thought of what she was doing she placed the medallion on his chest. "Power of the fae, I call to thee," she intoned softly, "strength to heal, lend to me."

The stone glowed red, spilling through her fingers, spreading like blood across Bern's chest. Vala was aware of the men moving, but she refused to break her concentration. If they came for her, so be it, but she would not let Bern die. The intensity of the stone changed, the red growing deeper and darker, covering Bern completely, then snaking out to touch Aric as well. Vala began to tremble, and nausea crept through her. Still, she clutched at the medallion, willing it to help Bern, to help Aric.

"Enough." The voice was cool, calm and commanding.

Vala sagged as a hand reached down and plucked the medallion away from her. She heard a small gasp from Lawanda, and she turned toward her friend, confused. But all she saw was Aric, now standing on white sands, no sign of his injuries present. He was staring at her in obvious awe and surprise, while beside him stood Severrani, who now held the medallion.

Vala's gaze shifted to the cliffs. No one was there. She looked back toward Bern, but he, too, had disappeared.

"I'm back in Talede?" she asked, her voice no more than a croak.

"You are." Severrani's voice was as cool as his touch had been, sending waves of pain through Vala's heart. There was no hint of emotion, no caring tone, no appreciation for healing Aric. He seemed as distant as he had that first day she'd met him. "Where's Lawanda? Bern...did he die?" she managed, not looking up.

There was a moment of silence, and Vala finally brought her gaze up to meet Severrani's. His eyes were blue, again reflecting the color of the sea at his back. Vala's tears spilled over.

"Please, Severrani, forgive them all," she sobbed. "They don't understand. Don't let them hurt Lawanda and Tyrs. Bring them here if you must, but don't let the hatred of the Revered and my uncle destroy them as well. Please."

"They injured Prince Aric," Severrani said. "They sought to kill you. Yet, you forgive them?"

"They don't understand," she said again, suddenly just very tired.

Severrani hunkered down in front of her. "And you do?"

"No," she admitted. "I don't. But I saw acceptance in Bern's eyes. And Tyrs and Lawanda. They accepted me and loved me for who I am, not for what I might be. And the people of Gannabrina, they worship the fae. They want them to come back. They miss them terribly. And....and I..." She choked on her sobs. "I miss them as well."

Severrani looked up the cliff face, as if he could see the forest and the men poised there, held suspended in time. "Tell me why I should not dispose of them all? Why I should not exact revenge on them for daring to injure the Prince of Larendalath?"

Vala looked up at him. "The hate has to stop somewhere."

Severrani studied her for a long time, as if trying to understand her words. Aric finally moved forward and placed one hand on the fae's shoulder.

"She's right, Severrani," he said quietly. "The people have been punished long enough. They only know the fae as evil. It's time to let them know us for the good we can do, the good that Vala just did in saving Bern's life."

"It wasn't your father who was killed by their fear," Severrani said tightly.

"No, it wasn't," Aric admitted. "But think what Gannabribriel was doing. He was reaching out to them, trying to show them what we can give to them. We can't condemn them all for the acts of a few. And it was a human, Vala's mother, who tried to help Gannabribriel."

Severrani looked at him, startled. His gaze slid back to Vala, then again to the cliff face. Vala reached out and took his hand, holding it tightly lest he try to pull away, surprised when he did not.

"If we only show them hate they will only react with fear," she said. "If we show them love, perhaps--perhaps they will react with acceptance."

"Perhaps?" he murmured.

"Isn't it at least worth a try? Gannabribriel tried. Would his son do any less?"

Severrani sighed, and straightened. Vala started as a groan suddenly came from the ground beside her. Her gaze snapped around, and a gasp escaped her. Bern was there, looking up at her as if no time had passed at all. Vala cast a quick glance around. Severrani and Aric were nowhere to be seen. And even though those who hated her now surrounded her, Vala had no great sense of fear. She suspected Severrani watched.

"Did you see that, Revered?" Hanlick whispered, his face a ghastly white. "The boy...he just disappeared. And...and Vala, she saved Bern's life."

"Took him as fae demon she did," the Revered mumbled, but his voice lacked conviction.

"No!" Tyrs shouted. "She used her magic and she saved him, saved him from what Odig did! If he had died it would not have been by Vala's hand. It was Odig and his hatred."

Bern got slowly to his feet, touching at his head in disbelief. "The Revered is wrong. Odig is wrong. I accept the fae for who they are. They're not demons." He swung his gaze to the other men. "Odig is wrong! Look at me! If the fae were demons would I be healed? Would I be standing here talking to all of you? Vala has done nothing to me, to us. Yet, we hunted her down like...like prey. I am ashamed of my actions. Ashamed. And so should all of you be."

"But what of the children?" one of the men demanded. "The fae take our children."

Bern sagged as if understanding what the others could not. "We did not accept them. And so they punished us." He turned to face Vala, then sank to his knees. "I beg your forgiveness, Vala. I vow, here and now, before you and the Gods, that I will no longer hunt the fae nor will I fear them. It is time to live in peace, time to heal the wounds, time for the children to come home."

Vala swallowed hard. "Don't bow before me, Bern. I am no god. I am only Vala, a woman born on the wrong side of the border."

Lawanda touched her arm, but at that moment, Vala was drawn back to Talede.

She looked at Severrani in confusion, but he seemed just as puzzled. It was Aric who broke the silence.

"Father!" he cried.

Vala whirled, surprised, even as Severrani fell to one knee, head bowed. He immediately removed his sword, laying it well away from him in the sand in an obvious gesture of subservience. A tall, broad-shouldered man strode toward them down the beach. He was clothed in fine silks adorned with silver braiding. A golden crown tamed white locks around a square-jawed face in which blue eyes smoldered with rage. One hand gripped a heavy staff, made of twisted wood and decorated with an assortment of jewels.

The Reth stormed up to Aric and, without a word, backhanded him hard enough to send the boy sprawling to the beach. Severrani flinched but did not regain his feet. The Reth whirled toward him.

"What is the meaning of this?" he roared. "What are you doing here? I did not ask you to assist Aric in any way. The task of returning this wayward whore was his and his alone."

Vala clenched her jaw in anger at the words. "I am not a whore!" The words came out before she could stop them.

The Reth turned on her in fury, stopping just short of striking her as well. He glared at her, his gaze raking over her features. The look was familiar, as if she had withstood its scrutiny before. She frowned, taking a step backward.

"Please, M'lord," Severrani said, "your anger at me is deserved, but Aric is--"

"Aric is nothing!" Etharid interrupted.

Aric wiped blood from his mouth and looked up at his father. "Then let me leave," he said quietly. "I'll go away, far away. You'll never have to set eyes on me again."

Etharid eyed him with contempt. "Would that I could, Aric. You have brought nothing but disgrace to the palace. You can't do anything right, not even the simple task of fetching a baby from the humans."

He flung out his hand, intending to strike Aric yet again, but Vala blocked his hand.

Startled, Etharid jerked aside. "How dare you touch me!"

Abandoning formalities and subservience, Severrani scrambled to his feet. "She is not fae, Your Majesty. Not truly. She was cursed by my father, and made to find her way to the Faery Realm. She does not know fae custom or courtesy."

"I am quite aware of who she is!" Etharid snapped, then turned his gaze on Vala again. "She is the cause of all the grief in Strander, all of the heartache and tears."

"No!" Aric cried. "No, she's not. How could it be her fault? She didn't ask to be saved from the faeries."

"Saved?" Etharid echoed. "It is not the faeries one needs saving from."

"Isn't it?" Vala asked. "My mother had always preached that the fae were supposed to be a benevolent race, yet all I have seen is rage and hatred. Even hatred for your own son!"

"Vala!" Severrani interrupted sternly. "That's enough! You are speaking to the king."

"He's not my king!" Vala retorted. "I wouldn't bow down to him by command or choice!"

Pure fury flashed through the Reth's eyes, and Vala was abruptly seized with gripping pain. It raged through her, tore into her senses, dropped her to her knees, gasping and shaking.

"Stop!" Severrani cried. "Please, M'lord, stop!"

"Leave her alone!" Aric shrieked, and leapt at his father.

Caught off-guard, the Reth tumbled to the beach, Aric atop him. The boy slammed his fist against Etharid's cheek in fury.

"I hate you!" he screamed, his anger unleashed in a flurry of wild punches. A second later, he was flung aside as if he were no more than a rag doll. He landed hard at the surf's edge, sending a spray of salty water onto

Vala and Severrani. The fae leapt forward, grabbed Aric by one arm and hauled him to his feet. With the other hand, he yanked Vala up and placed both of them behind him as Etharid also regained his feet.

"M'Lord," Severrani said, his voice shaking, "please calm yourself. It will accomplish nothing to strike out at those who do not know better."

"My son and my slaves are just that, Severrani! Mine!" Etharid roared. "And you are treading on very thin ground just now. Don't think I don't know what you've done in the past, how you shielded Aric from the pain of my punishments, how you took that pain on yourself." He suddenly stopped and glanced at Aric, a smug smile on his face. "You didn't know that did you? How Severrani suffered your punishments? Did you never wonder why you could not feel the full intensity of my magic?"

"I...I thought you were being lenient with me," Aric stammered. "B...because I was your son."

"Bah! I would kill you in a heartbeat if I had another to take your place! I may do so anyway. You're not worth the trouble of keeping you alive! You're certainly not worth the throne."

"Your Majesty!" Severrani gasped. "You cannot mean that. You're angry, your words are rash."

"My words are mine to speak as I will," the Reth snarled. "You are the High Healer of Larendalath, but that could change in a heartbeat. Don't forget it!"

Vala felt Severrani stiffen, and she looked past him to Etharid. Again, she was struck with the familiarity of the king's actions and words, particularly the way he brandished the heavy staff as he spoke.

"I have not forgotten my place, Your Majesty," Severrani said, tightly, "I am only asking for your mercy toward these two young people."

"Stand aside, Severrani!" the Reth boomed.

Vala shrieked as magic snaked out, lashing Severrani so fiercely that he was flung to one side. Etharid swung his staff in a hard, fast arc. It slammed against Aric's side with a sickening crack. The boy was too stunned to even cry out. He crumpled to the sands, the color draining from his face, even as his father struck him again, sending the heavy staff smashing into Aric's gut.

Vala threw herself atop him, taking the next blow on her own back and shoulders. She arched back with a scream of agony, as images flashed through her mind. Odig and Etharid mingled, combined, separated and combined again. How many times had she lay curled on the floor while her uncle wielded his cane against her young body? How many times had she begged for death over his torture? Just as she heard Aric murmuring now as he lay beneath her. And suddenly Vala knew.

"Odig!" The word left her lips in a disbelieving whisper. She twisted toward Severrani who had managed to regain his feet, and screamed, "Odig is Etharid."

Etharid started in outright surprise, and ceased his attack. He fell back a step, then gave her a cold smile. "You're very quick, for a human," he murmured. "And apparently very talented as well. I should have killed you when--"

"When? At the same time you killed Gannabribriel?" She managed to sit up, but kept one hand on Aric protectively. It was all clear now. Everything. It hadn't been Odig at all who had crushed Gannabribriel's skull. It had been Etharid in the guise of the old man. Vala knew it to be true beyond any doubt. "You killed Gannabribriel," she said again, her tone in quiet disbelief. "You pretended to be Odig, to make the villagers think it was Odig, but it was you." She turned her gaze on Severrani. "Read the medallion, Severrani. It's all there. Everything."

Etharid stiffened, his eyes narrowing to hate filled slits. "I am the fae king," he seethed. "It is my right, my power to do as I see fit."

"Then it's true?" Severrani breathed. "You killed my father?"

"It is my right," Etharid repeated, then slowly drew his sword. "As it is my right to kill his son. On your knees before me!"

Vala gasped in true horror, but it was Aric who reacted. He surged to his feet, Severrani's sword in his hand. With an enraged scream, he drove the sharp blade through Etharid's back. The tip of the weapon burst through the Reth's abdomen, spraying blood outward, even as Severrani's cry of disbelief echoed from the cliffs. Aric loosed a primal scream and twisted the sword as hard as he could, ensuring the thrust would be fatal.

Vala covered her mouth with her hands, her senses recoiling, as Etharid's fingers loosed their grip on his weapon and it fell to the ground. The Reth crumpled forward onto the sand.

"What have you done?" Severrani whispered.

Aric stared at his father's lifeless body, his young face empty of emotion. "The King is dead," he murmured, then sank to his knees. "Severrani, your dagger."

"Aric, what --" Vala started but was promptly shushed by Aric's impatient wave of his hand.

Vala watched as Severrani handed Aric the long, sharp dagger.

"Your hand then," Aric said.

"Aric, I am not sure you --"

Severrani was cut off with the same impatient motion, and he held his right hand up, palm facing Aric. The boy took a deep breath as if to steady himself, then sliced a long, clean line down Severrani's palm. The fae winced, his eyes closing momentarily in pain.

"Aric!" Vala cried, moving forward. "Stop! Don't."

But the boy ignored her, took the dagger and sliced across his own hand. Vala stared, confused, and repulsed, as Aric held his bleeding hand toward Severrani. "Pledge," Aric ordered.

"I pledge to you, King Aric," Severrani whispered, and clasped Aric's hand in his own.

At once, Aric crumpled, and Severrani caught him, cradling him gently in his arms. Vala rushed toward them, and watched in amazement as both wounds closed and healed in a matter of seconds. Understanding finally came. They had sealed an agreement, a pledge to each other, healer to king.

Aric looked up at her. "You'll come back to Larendalath with us," he said. It was not a question.

Vala swallowed hard, and nodded. She had no other choice.

Epilogue

Vala paused outside the door to the Healer's Chamber. A lot had happened since their return. News of Etharid's death had been received with a palpable sense of relief within the fae kingdom, and Aric had been eagerly accepted as the new King of Larendalath. Once back in full magic Severrani had used his remarkable gift to heal the boy's wounds. Vala had been awed to watch him work, though he told her that her gift was just as powerful as his. She doubted that, since she had to rely on the medallion as a crutch. Still, it made her feel good to hear the praise.

Aric had wasted no time in freeing the concubines to pursue their own lives, though most had elected to stay on at the palace under his rule. Aric had been flustered with that decision, until Severrani suggested that the women be assigned working tasks throughout the palace.

Aric had also insisted that Severrani keep his position of High Healer, which Vala knew both pleased and distressed the fae. If his yearning for

Gannabrina was even half as intense as hers, she knew his heartache at not being able to return. Still, he had pledged openly and freely to Aric, his new king. With a soft sigh, she opened the door and stepped into the Healer's Chambers.

Severrani rose at once from his desk, his gaze welcoming, though at the same time sad.

"Aric asked me to meet him here," Vala explained. "Do you know why?"

Severrani regarded her quietly, then reseated himself. "He told me that he had a matter of grave importance to discuss with you." He looked back at the various scrolls and parchments strewn on the hardwood desk, fiddling with his quill pen. "I--I believe he will ask your hand in marriage."

"Marriage!" Vala cried.

"Yes, King Aric thinks a great deal of you."

"Well, I care for him, too, but I don't love him!" Vala replied. "I mean, not in that way."

"He is the king, Vala."

"I don't care who he is!" Vala snapped. "I'll not marry a man I don't love!"

"I'm glad to hear that," Aric said, stepping into the room.

Severrani fell to one knee at once, his head bowed.

"Will you stop that?" Aric snapped good-naturedly.

"You are the fae king now," Severrani told him. "You must get used to--"

"I know, I know," Aric interrupted. "I must get used to all of the subservient gestures." He walked to Severrani and urged him to stand. "But not from you. And apparently not from Vala, either," he teased. "As for marrying--"

Vala whirled toward him, flushing. "Aric, I--I didn't mean that you..."

He held up one hand, silencing her. "I know what you meant." He pulled at a cord about his neck, drawing out the medallion.

Vala frowned, wondering why he still hadn't given it to Severrani. She could tell by the look in the fae's eyes that he longed to hold this remnant of his past life, this remembrance of his father.

"All right," Aric said. "I admit it took me a little while to figure out how to read the full story in the stone, but I finally did. I know everything now, everything that Gannabribriel placed into this bit of metal." He removed the medallion from about his neck, then reached for Severrani's hand. "I know who my mother was, Severrani."

"Do you?" the fae asked softly.

Aric placed the medallion on Severrani's palm and curled his fingers about it. "She was your mother as well."

Vala gasped, her gaze flying between the two fae. "You--you're brothers!"

Aric grinned. "Half-brothers by blood, full brothers by heart. Our mother loved Gannabribriel, but was forced by royal protocol to marry Etharid, to bring the kingdoms of Gannabrina and Larendalath together. When Etharid realized that she would never love him, that her heart belonged to Gannabribriel, he decided to remove Gannabribriel from the equation. By placing him in the human world and stripping him of his magic Etharid was able to kill him just as any mortal man. But he didn't know of Gannabribriel's strength through this medallion. He never suspected that the Elthea would place his history here, in this stone." He looked at Vala. "And he never thought that Gannabribriel would place one of his Chosen to watch over the medallion."

"Chosen?" Vala shook her head, confused. "But I thought it was a curse."

"So did I at first. But it isn't. It's more a blessing. Right Severrani?" He glanced at the elder fae. "That's why you were so shaken when she told you her name. The Chosen. The one who would bring the truth to Larendalath, to the fae."

Severrani paused, then nodded, his gaze on Vala. "Gannabribriel put a spell on you, that's true, but it was one to protect you. Etharid couldn't kill you in the human world, and he couldn't bring you here against your will. All he could do was to try to poison the minds of the other villagers against you in the hopes that one of them would kill you for him."

"Then that's why my uncle never killed me," Vala murmured. "Because he was Etharid." She shook her head. "But that doesn't make sense. I knew my uncle Odig. He used to come to our house when I was small. He was never comfortable around me because of what Gannabribriel did, but he was never cruel to me either. It was only after my parents died that he changed."

"I suspect that was when your uncle died, and was replaced by my father," Aric said quietly. He sighed, and sat down in Severrani's chair. "My father killed your uncle, Vala, so that he could take your uncle's place in the village. Since he could do nothing to mortally harm you himself, he tried to turn the other villagers against you. He appeared in your village just enough to keep the fires of anger and fear burning, and waited for you to come here where he thought he could have control over you."

"Then why didn't he?"

Aric chuckled, and glanced at Severrani. "Just another trick of Gannabribriel's. You were sort of invisible in the fae world. My father couldn't sense you here. It must have driven him to distraction. As Odig, he must have known you had crossed over, since he couldn't find you in the village. But he couldn't find you here either." He laughed again, obviously pleased that someone had actually outwitted the Reth. "Anyway, as much as he encouraged the villagers to make short work of you, they wouldn't. Seems your friend Lawanda is not one to toy with. Without Etharid around to poison their minds your people have begun to accept the fae. Perhaps not as openly as those people on Gannabrina, but it will happen. You'll see. It will happen."

Vala smiled, but mention of her head-strong and determined friend brought Vala's thoughts back to the babies. So far, neither Severrani nor Aric had talked of the situation. Vala wasn't sure she should mention it either, but she had to know. "So, why do the fae take the babies?"

"That was Etharid's doing," Aric said. "Part of his plan to instill fear, to blame you for everything evil. I didn't even know. I was told from the time I was young that the humans were our enemies, but I was never told why. I should have questioned it, I suppose, but I was too scared." His shoulders slumped in self-recrimination.

Vala winced, sensing his pain and guilt. "And now that you're king? Will the babies come back?"

The youth narrowed his eyes, and a sudden, small smile quirked his lips. His answer was evasive. "Well, I don't intend on taking any more children away from the village. Do you, Severrani?"

The elder fae started, but answered, his words measured and careful. "I must admit that I was never in favor of the past course of action regarding the children of Strander."

Aric frowned a moment, then grinned. "Oh! You mean you didn't like the way my father ran things?"

Severrani flushed. "I...well, I..."

It was the first time Vala had seen the fae at a loss for words, and somehow it made him all the more appealing to her. She started to giggle despite herself. Severrani's gaze shot to her in surprise, then to Aric, when he, too, began to chuckle.

"That is not what I said!" Severrani stated.

"Oh? So you liked the way my father ran things then?" Aric countered, then dissolved into gales of laughter at the look that crossed Severrani's face. Finally, the youth calmed, and took Severrani by the arm, his tone now serious. "Our mother died of a broken heart, Severrani. There is nothing I can do to change that, but there is much I can do to make sure that her son does not die of a broken heart as well."

Severrani frowned warily. Aric's smile broadened, as if he harbored a great and special secret.

"I know how you feel about Gannabrina," Aric continued. "I know how Vala feels about it. And," he added, with a mischievous twinkle in his eyes, "I know how you two feel about each other, despite your clumsy attempts to deny it."

Vala felt the color rush to her cheeks, and she dared a glance at Severrani. He quickly averted his gaze, his own cheeks a matching red. Aric laughed out loud, obviously quite happy with the awkward position he'd thrust Severrani and Vala into.

"It's not as if you didn't make it obvious," Aric continued. "Vala was always watching your eyes, Severrani. You were always watching her. That excuse about walking to Larendalath through the meadows and the desert wasn't even a good one. Walking! You? Please. It was only done so you could spend more time getting to know Vala. Admit it."

Severrani stared at him. "I...I..."

"And Vala," Aric went on, obviously enjoying himself immensely, "she never wanted to leave you in the first place. I practically had to drag her back to Lareriveth. All she thought about was leaving you alone, and unprotected, in the desert, even after she'd witnessed your magic." He shook his head, chuckling. "And all of those tender touches...the finger, the hair, the..."

"Your point, M'Lord?" Severrani interrupted, though his voice cracked.

Aric's eyebrows rose in amusement. "Just this. You need to be together. It was obvious from the start. Therefore, I pledge you as husband and wife."

Vala sucked in her breath, almost afraid to look at Severrani. When she did, she found him staring at her, his blue eyes soft and questioning.

Aric nudged Severrani with his elbow. "Oh, for the love of the fae! Seal this betrothal. Kiss her!"

Severrani hesitated only a moment. "He is my king," he whispered. "I cannot defy him."

Vala winced. "Do you want to?" she asked.

A small smile touched at his lips. "No," he whispered. He leaned forward, and touched gently at her lips.

Though the kiss was brief and gentle, it sent a delightful, warm tingle shooting through her.

"There!" Aric announced. "Now that that's settled, there's someone here to see you, Vala." He moved toward the doors, and opened them, motioning to someone beyond.

Vala gasped in astonishment as Vaedon and Aerawin slipped shyly into the room, followed by their parents. Elaewen held a chubby toddler at her hip. Laraliwyn. She was even more beautiful than Vala remembered her. Her gaze flew to Aric. "How... where..."

"Faery!" Vaedon cried, abandoning all pretenses at decorum. He rushed across the room and flung himself into her arms. Aerawin was close behind.

"By the Saints!" Vala breathed. "How I've missed you! Look how you've both grown! How handsome, how beautiful you are."

"Not as pretty as you," Vaedon said quietly.

Vala blushed, then moved toward Elaewen and Frayhan, and reached out to touch the baby's soft, red hair. Laraliwyn gurgled happily, her blue eyes sparkling. Vala looked back at Aric. "How did you find them?"

"It was easy," Aric told her. "You met Ybrilla, didn't you?"

"Yes, but I don't see--"

"Ybrilla!" Severrani interrupted, in obvious surprise. "I've known her since I was a small child. How did you meet her?"

Vala turned to Frayhan, but he merely shrugged. "I had my suspicions about Ybrilla, so when Vala asked for answers to her questions, I brought Ybrilla to her. Apparently my suspicions proved to be correct."

"We have only one faery in Gannabrina," Vaedon interrupted. "We need more. And you said you would come back." He yanked a chain out from hiding beneath his tunic. Vala recognized it at once. Obviously so did Severrani, as a soft gasp escaped him.

"That was my father's," he said quietly.

"Your father's?" Vaedon asked, obviously puzzled. "But I kept it safe for Vala. I took very good care of it." He removed the chain and handed it to Vala.

She looked up at Severrani, who took the chain from her hands. He stroked the silver thoughtfully, then suddenly replaced the chain about Vaedon's neck.

"You have safe kept the chain all these months," the fae said. "I can see no better place for it to remain."

Vaedon looked up at him in astonishment. "I can keep it?" he breathed.

Severrani smiled. "Yes, you may keep it." He cocked his head thoughtfully, his gaze moving to Aerawin, who wore a look of disappointment. Severrani smiled, removed the chain from Vaedon's neck, then passed one hand over it, murmuring soft words. Now, in his hand, were two chains, exactly the same length. He placed one about Vaedon's neck, the other about Aerawin's. The little girl squealed with delight, as Severrani straightened.

"Consider it a payment for watching over my lovely wife-to-be," he said.

The familiar butterflies returned to Vala's stomach, but this time they seemed to be dancing. She looked up at Severrani, sinking once more into his blue eyes.

"Your wife?" Vaedon echoed. He looked back at Vala. "You're getting married?"

"Yes, it's settled," Aric proclaimed. "We leave within the week for Gannabrina."

"What?" Severrani's gasp mingled with Vala's.

Aric rolled his eyes and winked at Vala. "He's been around you too long. He's beginning to repeat everything I say," he teased, then continued. "My mother was from Gannabrina. It is as much my land as Larendalath is. There is nothing that says that I must rule from here, is there?"

"No!" Severrani answered at once, as if the thought had never occurred to him. "No, there isn't."

"Yippee!" Aerawin shrieked, clapping her hands. "The faery is coming back, and she's getting married. Now, there'll be lots and lots of faeries in Gannabrina, because they'll have lots and lots of babies."

Vala felt the color rush to her cheeks, and she shot a glance at Severrani. He was regarding her in open astonishment. "I...I suppose that's true," he managed. "If...if Vala agrees, that is."

Vala swallowed hard. "Babies?" she mused. "I guess I never thought about ever becoming a mother."

"And now?" Severrani asked.

"Now? Now, it sounds like the most wonderful thing in the whole world."

Severrani smiled, and reached for her hands. She gave them, her heart fluttering in anticipation. She started when Aric cleared his throat.

"Speaking of babies," he said. "There's something else I wanted you to see, Vala." He took her by the hand and led her to a mirror that hung on one wall.

Severrani followed, as did the children.

"Watch this, Severrani," Aric said proudly. "I've been practicing my magic." He gestured at the mirror. It misted over, then abruptly cleared. Vala recognized the scene at once. It was the Funeral Meadow outside of Strander. Wildflowers bloomed with wild abandon, turning the hillside into a riot of color, seeming to celebrate the lives of those who slept peacefully beneath them. As she watched, Tyrs came into view, laughing and motioning to someone behind him. Lawanda caught up with him, smiling, one hand at the small of her back, the other on a protruding belly. Vala whirled to Aric, tears forming in her eyes. "The children," she whispered.

"Aye," he said. "And she carries not one, but two, as a special gift from the fae. And, this time, all of the children will live. All of them.

Vala's sob of relief escaped her, and, without thinking, she grabbed Aric in a fierce hug. "Thank you! Thank you, from the bottom of my heart!"

"Oh, look!" Aerawin cried, pointing at the mirror. "It's snowing!"

Vala released her hold on Aric, and turned to the mirror. Aric crossed his arms over his chest, a smug smile of satisfaction on his lips. Lawanda and Tyrs stood in the meadow, their shocked faces tilted skyward. Thousands of white flower petals fluttered through the air, drifting gently down upon the meadow grasses and wildflowers. Lawanda suddenly smiled, then kissed her palm and threw the kiss skyward, her lips moving in speech. And even though Vala could not hear her words, she knew what they were, for Severrani leaned close to her ear and repeated them.

"I love you, Vala Kalei. I love you."

You can find ALL our books up on our website at:

http://www.writers-exchange.com

all our fantasy novels:

http://www.writers-exchange.com/category/genres/fantasy/

JennaKay Francis has been writing since she was 12 years old. She has written in many different genres - science fiction, childrens, mainstream, poetry - but truly found her voice and love in fantasy. She writes fantasy adventure, fantasy romance, dark fantasy and children's picture books.

Her first official publication was a children's poem that was the Grand Prize winner in a contest sponsored by Half-Price Books. Her prize was a $500.00 gift certificate at Half Price Books: something she took great delight in spending. She has been published in several local newsletters, several print magazines, as well as numerous online magazines in both fiction and non-fiction.

Jenna lives in the beautiful Pacific Northwest with her husband, their three delightful children, two wild cats, a chihuahua that thinks he's really a dog, one rat, one anole and a several tanks of tropical fish, frogs and newts. Oh, yeah, and a forest full of elves, fairies and magic.

JennaKay was also Writers Exchange's Senior editor for many years. You can keep track of all her books on her author page:

http://www.writers-exchange.com/Jennakay-Francis/

If you want to read more about other books by this author, they are listed on the following pages...

Blood Bred Series

{Fantasy: Vampire}

Book 1: Gift of Blood

Jaeger needs blood. Half Vector, half human, newly coming of age, Jaeger is now drawn to human blood for the first time in his already long life.

Rhiannon, a witch, has too much iron in her blood to safely live. She wants to propose a partnership with the Vectors, but, before she can approach them, she's attacked and left for dead beneath a pier. Jaeger finds her unconscious and bleeding. Fighting against the lure of her blood, he takes her to a place of safety instead. His actions set them both on a course of pain, hunger, terror and love. Can he save her from himself?

Publisher: http://www.writers-exchange.com/Gift-Of-Blood/

Book 2: From the Heart

Baris has everything: A wife he worships, a child he adores, a life of comfort and security. But his idyllic existence changes suddenly and dramatically, with no explanation. Anika, his wife, shuns him and orders him to leave her side. His child claims his mother is not really his mama. And Dierdre, a devastatingly beautiful young woman slides into Baris' life with seduction on her mind.

When Baris attempts to help his wife, she flees, leaving him alone with their son and Dierdre. To add to his agony, the child is bitten by a poisonous snake and Baris has no choice but to take him to the Lair to save his life. Once reunited with Dierdre, the pair set off in search of Anika. But, as the days turn to weeks with no sign of his wife, Baris must accept the possibility that she has no wish to be found.

As his life grows increasingly entangled with Dierdre's, he makes the mistake of feeding on a young man addicted to a powerful drug called Hack.

Baris is soon addicted as well and must struggle to reclaim everything that he once held dear...or die.

Publisher: http://www.writers-exchange.com/From-the-Heart/

Book 3: New Beginnings

A powerful Vector roams the dark alleys and streets searching for his next victim. But he he's not interested in those with normal blood--only those whose veins runs blood thick with the highly-addictive drug Hack. If Adan can't find someone who's just ingested the potent drug, he has no compunction about using his powers to coerce them to do so before he feeds.

For Vector Sovereign Darius, Adan has become a problem he needs to fix...

Publisher: http://www.writers-exchange.com/New-Beginnings/

Free Spirit

{Fantasy Romance}

Diesa de Tyronmen escapes from a brutal master only to be sold to an elf. Though mesmerized by his beauty, Diesa struggles for her freedom...and against her own growing love for her new master. Was she purchased only to win a wager? And, as her mother had claimed, will an elf claim her heart with his words, her very soul with his touch?

Publisher: http://www.writers-exchange.com/Free-Spirit/

Guardians of Glede Universe: Beginnings Series

{Fantasy: Young Adult}

When the balance of power is threatened in the land of Glede, the powerful Triskelion calls for its master.

Book 1: The Triskelion

The Triskelion, a powerful magical amulet, once torn into two parts to protect the world of Glede, now must be found and re-united to save Glede. Two boys are summoned by the magic of the Triskelion to perform this dangerous task -Treyas Beckering, a 14 year old elf from Bailiwycke in the west; and 13 year old Jannson van Tannen, the newly orphaned King of Odora Dava to the east. Both will endure more than they ever thought possible, and both will become men in the process.

Publisher: http://www.writers-exchange.com/The-Triskelion/

Book 2: Dark Prince

Prince Rugan Merripen, once thought to be the rightful master of the Triskelion's magic, was cast aside by the medallion itself when it chose his half-brother Treyas Beckering as master. Now Rugan is on a quest to regain the magic and power he thinks is rightfully his. Befriended and manipulated by Vaalde, an evil sorcerer who has only his own goals in mind, Rugan attempts to drain Glede of elfin magic. Once gone, only sorcery magic will remain and Vaalde can then rule the world. It is up to King Jansson and Treyas to stop him and restore the balance of magic once again. Each boy will face what seem to be insurmountable odds, and both will discover that friends are there to depend on in times of travail. And Treyas will move towards a destiny that he never envisioned.

Publisher: http://www.writers-exchange.com/Dark-Prince/

Book 3: Sorcerer's Pool

Firmly embedded into Prince Rugan's mind, the sorcerer Vaalde once more manipulates Prince Rugan into wresting the Triskelion magic from Treyas Beckering Merripen, now the Crown Prince of Lidgerwood. This time Vaalde spirits King Jansson van Tannen and Treyas to Karsaba, a land void of magic and the ability to drain memory. Three days outside of magic and their memories will be wiped clean. Unfortunately for Vaalde, King Kyel Sylvain has hitched a ride. The black elf, reknowned for his magical prowess will prove to be a formidable adversary. But will Jansson and Treyas survive the strange power of Karsaba or will they lose everything that makes them who they are?

Publisher: http://www.writers-exchange.com/Sorcerers-Pool/

Book 4: Dragons of Mere Odain

Far away in the land of Mere Odain, a dragon calls out for help to her master--Pepin Merripen, now living as the son of Crown Prince Treyas Merripen and his wife, Cynthe. Pepin must answer, or die. Shocked and terrified, Treyas gathers his closest friends, and goes to Mere Odain. But the country is in turmoil. An ethnic cleansing is going on--any black or brown skinned person must die. Treyas is determined to save his young son's life even if it means taking on the whole of the Keltin Empire and ending a war 40 years in the making.

Publisher: http://www.writers-exchange.com/Dragons-of-Mere-Odain/

Book 5: Dragon Master

Pepin Merripen learns that the two countries that had promised to protect the dragons, his dragons, have withdrawn their forces. Furious at this betrayal, he goes to Karsaba to take council with Mere Odain's young Queen. Although his father is willing to let Pepin resolve this situation, he soon finds out that Pepin has disappeared. Treyas follows his son's trail, but it ends where magic begins.

Increasingly worried, Treyas attempts to follow the magical trail and ends up in Northern Karsaba. It soon becomes apparent that he has more to deal with than a disgruntled runaway youth. A powerful magiker claiming to be Pepin's birth mother has summoned him, and she will stop at nothing to see his control over the dragons become her own. With Pepin at her command, and thereby his dragons, she intends to rule not only Karsaba, but any land she chooses. It is up to Treyas and his friends to make sure that doesn't happen. But will Treyas lose his son to the powerful pull of the dragons? Publisher: http://www.writers-exchange.com/Dragonmaster/

Book 6: For the Love of Dragons

Pepin Merripen, now a young man of fourteen, has forged a strong bond with the elves. So when Queen El'leigh of Mere Odain informs him that the dragons have disappeared, he is torn between his allegiance and his love for the dragons. Still, he is steadfast in his loyalty to his father, Treyas Merripen, and refuses El'leigh's request to join her in the search.

Furious, El'leigh sends Pepin's love, Nila, to the wilds of South Kelta, the last known place of the dragons. As she suspected, Pepin quickly follows before any harm befalls Nila. No sooner have the two young lovers arrived in Kelta, than they are captured by Keltin warriors, who quickly ascertain that they have the DragonMaster in their grasp. And if they can force Pepin to make the dragons do their bidding, they'll regain their lost advantage in Mere Odain. All they have to do is use Nila as incentive.

Publisher: http://www.writers-exchange.com/For-The-Love-Of-Dragons/

The Faery Sickness

{Fantasy Romance}

Vala Kalei was saved from death by the fae but condemned by her own neighbors. When she goes to the faery realm and retrieves the babies that have been dying, she opens up another world filled with mystery, pain, heartache...and love.

Publisher: http://www.writers-exchange.com/The-Faery-Sickness/

Guardians of Glede Universe Continued: Next Generation Series

{Fantasy: Young Adult}

Return to the land of Glede for new adventures with the next generation!

Book 1: Caves of Challenge

Their heads filled with stories of adventures spun by their father and uncles, Princes Vantann and Thomlin Merripen decide to have an adventure of their own. Through an old book, they learn of the Caves of Challenge. If they can survive the challenges within the caves, they will emerge as men.

Blackmailed by their young friend, Shuri, the boys agree to take her along. Before they trio has a chance to adequately prepare, however, they are sent to the Caves by haphazard magic. Once there, Shuri and Vantann are captured by War Gnomes, while Thomlin is lost in a dark swamp. His only consolation is that, somehow, he has snagged King Jansson van Tannen on the magic strand.

Jansson is reassuring, telling Thomlin that there will be a rescue party sent out and all they need do is wait. But the rescue party is having trouble of their own, and they find much more than they bargained for in the Caves. The question now becomes, who will be forced to stay in the Caves of Challenge forever.

Publisher: http://www.writers-exchange.com/Caves-of-Challenge/

Book 2: Blood Sacrifice

Tormented with guilt over the happenings in the Caves of Challenge, Prince Vantann Merripen watches over his siblings with a critical, judgmental and sometimes violent scrutiny. Prince Thomlin finally rebels and accidentally sets the course for an even more dangerous adventure than the one he and his brother endured in the Caves. Swept into a land that demonizes the second-born of twins, forbids magic, and is currently being terrorized by a coven of Nydiri, the twins very survival is threatened.

Any use of magic carries the penalty of death. Contact with the coven means the same, for the Nydiri are actively seeking twins to complete a powerful spell they intend to weave at the height of a mysterious orange moon. And elvin twins are especially prized.

Publisher: http://www.writers-exchange.com/Blood-Sacrifice/

Book 3: The Coven

Pepin reclaims his title as DragonMaster, not fully understanding the ramifications of such a move. Is his allegiance with the elves, or with Mere Odain? The announcement of his decision couldn't have come at a worse time – the Crown Prince is to leave the next day on a diplomatic visit to Dalziel.

Once in Dalziel, things rapidly begin to fall apart. Politically, Kyel and Jansson are at each other's throats, Vantann and Thomlin make friends in the wrong places, and Treyas finds out that his SoulMate and squire, Druce Sinclair, suffers from a horribly painful and incurable disease.

To top it off, Treyas discovers that Dalziel has been overrun with Nydiri with the power of Illusion in their grasp.

When Vantann, Thomlin and others disappear, Treyas must find a way to free the captives and destroy the Nydiri threat once and for all...

Publisher: http://www.writers-exchange.com/The-Coven/

Book 4: Fire Stone

Stranded after a river float trip goes horribly wrong, Brann van Tannen and his friends Tavin, Elek and Janna are caught by slave traders. To make matters worse, on board the barge are three trolls, descendants of the tribe that destroyed Mayfaire and killed Brann's grandfather. Brann will need to rely on all of the strength, wisdom and courage his father instilled in him while their lives are changed beyond wildest imagination.

Publisher: http://www.writers-exchange.com/Fire-Stone/

Book 5: The Fane Queen

Attempting to escape the past can have devastating consequences...

Ask Tavin Sylvain, who is trying to forget all about the abuse he suffered at the hands of the trolls six months earlier.

Ask Kitiara, who would like to escape her sordid past in Kartonn, where she was known as the Princess of Pleasure.

Or ask King Jansson van Tannen, who would like nothing better than to keep his family intact and not have to face the possibility of losing one of his own beloved children to fate.

When the past rears its ugly head, all three are thrown into turmoil. Tavin, Brann and Kitiara are lost in Karsaba, without magic, without direction, without hope. And in the middle of a troll invasion. In a race against time, King Jansson and King Kyel gather their closest friends and allies to find the children before the trolls find them first.

Publisher: http://www.writers-exchange.com/The-Fane-Queen/

Book 6: Battle for Argathia

A desperate plea for help, written on a scroll and sent with magic, falls into the wrong hands, and with a few misplace words, Treyas' young daughter activates the spell, sending her and her friends to a world controlled by the Albino.

The Albino, not content with being dictator of only one world, now has a hostage--and one of royal pedigree--with which to extend his empire. It is up to Treyas and his companions to stop the Albino and free the world he has claimed as his own.

Publisher: http://www.writers-exchange.com/Battle-for-Argathia/

Guardians of Glede Universe Continued: Reckonings Series

{Fantasy: Young Adult}

Return to the land of Glede during a time when the Nydiri intend to destroy not only Treyas but the whole of the elven empire.

Book 1: Dukker's Revenge

Elek is missing and Dukker has returned. The Nydiri will not stop until not only Treyas is destroyed but the whole of the elven empire. When the palace is infiltrated, chaos ensues. Floy, the son of a visiting dignitary, becomes an unwitting pawn in Dukker's plans. Through him, Dukker captures three of the royal youth.

Treyas and his companions set out to rescue the young people, but their TravelSpell is severely compromised, sending them in different directions. They will all need to rely on new friends, and a powerful, mysterious dagger, to set things right and defeat the Nydiri.

Publisher: http://www.writers-exchange.com/Rukkers-Revenge/

Nitesh

{Fantasy Romance}

Thalassa, a sea-witch, is captured when the warlord Rhaeven sends his troops to her small village. After the hard life she's already lived, she's resigned to her fate. Married at a young age to an abusive man she doesn't love, she's secretly glad to see her husband die. Now, pregnant, enslaved and stricken with a deadly disease, she only waits for her own death to release her from the torment that is life.

Elfin Crown Prince of Diraenia, Terran, must choose a mate and produce an heir before his thirtieth birthday or risk forfeiting the crown to his youngest brother Unwin. Time is running out. Terran is twenty-nine, his fiancee is dead, and he believes Unwin responsible despite the lack of proof. To make matters worse, Terran's other brother Sinclair has disappeared, and Terran fears the worst.

Bothered by a strange, haunting beat of drums no one can hear but Terran, the Crown Prince thoughts continually turn to a brief encounter he shared with a young woman from Zal. For three days, he'd walked her back to her village, delivering her to her pre-ordained life there. For three days, he fell in love with the wife of a woman who could never be his. When he returned to his own palace, he'd seen the emptiness and despair of his own life.

The drums call to Terran until he can longer deny his own need to revisit the village where he'd fallen in love. If he sees Thalassa one last time, can he make himself let go?

Publisher: http://www.writers-exchange.com/Nitesh/